Material

LEFT AT THE ALTAR

III

RAINE MILLER

Raine Miller Romance

Copyright © 2018 *Raine Miller Romance*
All rights reserved.
Cover Design: Jena Brignola
Cover Image: Scott Hoover
Cover Model: Sonny Henty
Editing: Marion Archer

ISBN-13: 978-1725709782
ISBN-10: 1725709783

DEDICATION

To the guy who believes I wrote this story just for him.

Fantasies are a wonderful thing.

ACKNOWLEDGMENTS

THANK YOU TO JAN FOR INVITING me to be part of her wonderful project brainchild: **_Left at the Altar_**. I have enjoyed every minute of this amazing collaboration. As well as many heartfelt thanks to my series partners on this fun adventure: **J.S. Scott, Ruth Cardello, Sawyer Bennett, Minx Malone, Melody Anne,** you ladies rock it every single day and I am honored to have been a part of this with you.

A very special thank you goes out to Niloufer for her generous assistance with the French translations for Giselle. _xo Merci chérie._

XO RAINE

PROLOGUE

Gage,

This is me breaking up with you. Enclosed is the ring that you made me pick out—alone. The same ring-choosing at Tiffany's you were an hour and ten-minutes late for.

Yes, that's right, Gage, my dear uncaring asshat fiancé. I've left you, and this godforsaken beach shithole.

We've reached the natural progression of all our fights, all your pointed silences, all your lame excuses. By now, it has to be fifty going on a hundred times you've sworn to change, sworn you're trying to open up to me. But I think we both know the indifferent mask you wear has become so ingrained it's a part of you now.

Not to mention your <u>zero</u> consideration for me. You should know what I'm going to say here—because in the last two years, how many millions of occasions have I asked you to put your dirty socks in the hamper? But you haven't even been *able to do that simple little thing. Asshole.*

And yes, what I found this morning—determined the end of this shitshow of a relationship. The sock that broke the loveless relationship's back. Fitting, in a sad way. Dirty weed-green socks flung in actual sneezing distance of the wicker hamper—the very one I bought with an easy-open lid just for you. I stared at those disgusting dirty socks and decided that I didn't want to do this anymore. Not with you.

Because let's face it, this isn't just about socks. This is about respect. The respect you do not have for me, or my feelings in any way, shape, or form. But that's understandable considering your cold heart barely beats even on a good day. So, I've decided it's much better to do this now instead of later.

Gage Danielson, I will not go through with a farce of a marriage like the one you proposed only from of a dull sense of duty. Paul and Isa's wedding breaking down at the altar last month was like a last-minute-rescue-mission-wake-up call for me. I've realized I don't have to do this <u>with you</u> anymore. I don't have to marry a man who won't ever love me the way I deserve to be loved. You aren't husband material any more than your neurotic friend Paul is.

Unlike you, work isn't my life. My life is <u>my</u> life, and I intend to keep it that way. And I intend to spend it with a man who loves me.

Get ready for this next part.

You know your friend Parker? Well, you successfully managed to ignore me so much that I ended up making him my friend too. The kind of friend you have naked sleepovers with.

I would say I'm sorry and wish you the best, but let's not lie to each other.

Not every man has what's necessary to be husband material. And since you're definitely not one of them, I guess you'd better get used to being alone...forever.

-Cassidy

CHAPTER 1

"The worst part is that she's right."

I put my head in my hands.

Before Gray could respond, I continued. "Near the end, it did get pretty bad. But still, I didn't see *this train wreck* coming."

Gray ran a hand through his light brown hair, his eyes set obliquely to the left. "Must've been crazy rough, having to cancel that five-hundred-guest wedding she'd arranged down to the last pink peony and everything…"

"Don't remind me."

Gray had been one of the intended guests—my best man, in fact. He, along with Paul, and Reid, my other friends, and of course, good old Parker—trusted friend/fiancée stealer/MIA asshole of the year.

My hands clasped into tensed fists on the table. *How long?* Cassidy said she'd finally given up on us that morning, so exactly how long had they been having their *naked sleepovers?* I shouldn't really give a fuck, but what—? Had the idiot planned to accept Cassidy as my wife *and* still fuck her on the side? He's more of a moron than I thought possible. A look around the restaurant provided nothing in the way of interesting distraction for me. Everything was too dully recognizable, from the cheery streams of sunlight filtering in through the wide-open windows to the faces of the patrons it illuminated. Vaguely familiar faces looking just as delighted to be here as I wasn't.

Sure, it was good to see Gray, but the past weeks had been nothing short of hell on earth. Concerned calls from those I considered "close" alternating with judgmental and fucking obnoxious inquiries from far-off relations, and *barely* friends of my ex-fiancée streaming in on the regular.

My parents and I weren't on speaking terms over it, and Cassidy had been true to her word. After her spiteful letter, I hadn't heard a single bitchy peep from her. Which I guess was good, all things considered. She'd actually disappeared from Charleston entirely. Was apparently sunning it up in

5

Barbados with her asshole beau, which explained fuckhead Parker's absence.

I tossed some water down my throat, careful not to slam the glass on the table with the anger I felt. "A fucking letter?" I swigged the ice around in my glass listlessly. "I guess I shouldn't be surprised I got the most overdramatic letter from a failed actress."

Gray poured me some more water. "Please take comfort she did this *before* the ceremony, and you weren't in a tux in front of five hundred watchful wedding guests like Paul. You dodged that mess, at least.

I smiled bitterly. "It's the little things, true. Just wish it wasn't my so-called *friend* who took my girl, you know?"

"But did you really think of Cassidy as *your* girl, Gage? Not to be an asshole, but from where I was standing, she didn't make you happy. She was never…easygoing or…friendly."

I got that Gray was trying his best to be diplomatic in saying that my ex was a fucking bitch *most* of the time. *Honestly, I haven't mourned her departure. Have enjoyed the silence.* He should, because diplomatic skills were burned into his DNA. Grayson T. Lash III was the grandson of a former POTUS and the current Attorney General of the great state of South Carolina. To me, he was just my friend since as long as I could remember. I shook my head, my eyes going to the corner of this place. Jazz Street, it was called. There was no actual jazz here and, to my knowledge, there never had been in its long and illustrious history, dating back a good hundred years. But Jazz Street did have good food, windows that looked toward the beach, and a decent wine list.

Gray and I had come here more times than I could remember, right to this vaulted-ceiling corner with the slightly tippy table. Our usual spot for catching up on the latest news in our lives. He'd heard all about the perpetual Cassidy issues that had plagued my life over the last two years, so I figured it was past fucking time to find a new topic of conversation with one of my best friends, who also happened to be married to my cousin, Reese.

"She's definitely right about one thing," I said suddenly. "I'm not husband material, and I think I'm meant to be single. For good."

Chin in his hand, Gray tilted his head toward me, raising a brow.

"I mean it." I chomped on an ice cube, annoyed. Already, I could guess what Gray's reaction would be. "I know how things ended up working out for you and Reese, but that's not in the cards for me. I thrive on working hard and, to be honest, I probably haven't viewed any of my relationships as more than a convenience for getting laid." *And I can't even remember the last time Cassidy and I fucked.*

Over the rim of his crystal glass, Gray regarded me. "Has it ever occurred to you that you haven't met the right person yet?"

I shrugged. "With the number of women I've been with? No."

The other part I didn't mention to him. That last line of Cassidy's hatefully penned rant, the one telling me to enjoy being alone forever. Reading that part had sent a shiver through me like the unmistakable precision of a very sharp fucking blade. An omen of sorts.

My gaze absently left our table and spanned the familiar faces arranged within the white-walled, white-floored room. There was my old gym teacher, Mr. Cho Mi, with the perfectly spherical bald spot on his hair and too-bright, darting eyes. There was Laney, one of the many girls I'd dated, doing her best to keep her pointy chin turned well away from me. There was even a third cousin of mine, Paulina, who also wasn't looking at me, since she'd taken Cassidy's side in our breakup—for reasons that still escaped me, since they'd spoken to each other all of maybe two times.

As I sucked on an ice cube, my gaze snagged on one of the last people I wanted to see.

Mrs. Bardot—aka—Cassidy's mom, whose stick up her ass was roughly the same size as her daughter's. Her chlorine-colored eyes locked on me with nothing short of absolute hatred. Perhaps I should have paid more attention to her, given that the apple certainly hadn't fallen far from the tree. *And why the fuck is she angry with me? Cassidy fucked off and stopped the wedding.*

I emptied the rest of my water glass. "Think it's time to hit the waves."

Gray shifted uneasily in his seat. "You okay?"

I felt my brows knit in irritation. I'd always liked Gray's no-bullshit attitude. But ever since he and Reese had gone all BMCF—my business partner, Reid's cheeky invention, Best Married Couple Forever—he'd reached obnoxious heights of openness and transparency.

Which meant that right now, he was annoying the shit out of me by asking a question I didn't want to answer.

"You know, it's been four weeks since the letter." I picked up a napkin, tossed it up a few inches, then let it fall. "It still feels like yesterday."

I squared my shoulders as I rose.

There. I hadn't told the *I'm fine* lie. The one, which in the past month, had become my refrain to the point of sounding glib. But I hadn't told the truth either. I was fucking weeks, probably years away from *fine*. Because although I didn't miss Cassidy and knew I could get laid easily enough if I bothered to go out and find someone for the night, I didn't want to be alone forever. *Which is possibly why I asked her to marry me in the first place. Idiot.*

"Gage," Gray said sharply.

He smiled apologetically. "I am sorry. But you may want to stick around for another fifteen minutes or so."

I eyed him warily. "Why?"

He glanced at the door, then back at me. "It was Reid's idea. Lena's fresh out of her divorce, so we thought maybe that you two could…"

I shook my head. "Oh *hell*, no."

I'd heard enough horror stories through Reid to know that his psycho half-sister, no matter how chastised from her failed marriage she may have been, was the last thing I needed.

Demanding and *over the top* were not things that would make me a happy camper right now.

"Sorry, man." I tossed two twenties on the table. "But I've got to go. Glad we could meet while you were in town."

I barely gave him time to say "Bye, Gage" before my legs rapidly weaved me past rows of round tables toward the door. I was practically through its heavy frame when I nearly collided with her.

Lena raised her drawn-on eyebrows at me, to which I gave her a curt nod. She's lucky she'd even got that before I continued out the fucking door, the adrenaline ricocheting inside me fueling me forward.

Most of my relationship with Cassidy had been on her terms, and I wasn't about to subject myself to that doomed experiment again. Over the course of the time we'd been together, Cassidy and I'd *enjoyed* weekly yell-fests, monthly breakup threats, and quarterly out-and-out walkouts. Cassidy had also been especially skilled at meticulously outlining every single one of my faults.

Faults, which, as it turned out, were as numerous as the fucking stars in the solar system…apparently. *Fucking socks on the floor?* All her complaints had circled back to one overarching theme: I hadn't let my guard down with her, and I hadn't truly appreciated her.

Heading to my Mercedes-Maybach with the wise owl of hindsight on my shoulder, I had to admit it was possible that she'd had a point there. Whatever the case though, she should've made up her mind then—either accepted me for the disappointment I was—or left me a long fuckin' time ago. *And it now makes me wonder if Parker is the first? Ah, who gives a fuck.*

Finally inside my car, I closed my eyes and pictured the beckoning vista of blue that awaited me to help me calm down before I started driving. When I opened them a minute later, I wasted no time in heading out. It was a twenty-minute drive to Folly Beach in low traffic, and no way did I want to be thinking of my dearly departed, bitchy ex for the duration.

That was harder than it should be, though. This whole area was haunted by her to some degree— because we'd lived here together for two years.

And yet, Charleston was *my place*, had been since I was a kid. As easy as it would have been to leave, it felt like there was something wordless tying me

11

here—something like unfinished business. Or maybe it was because this was the only home I'd known, and that I'd designed the beach house I now lived in. Or rather in my ex's words: *this godforsaken beach shithole*. Again, I should be offended, but what-the-fuck-ever.

Its location right on Folly Beach was perfect for surfing when I wasn't working. No way would I give that up because the woman I'd made the mistake of trying to build a life with had decided I wasn't husband material. She hadn't minded my money though. Cassidy had liked to spend it with gusto, so I hoped that fucker Parker was up to the challenge of credit limit increases on his Amex. I think the real beginning-of-the-end came when I asked her to sign the prenup. I'm not that dumb. I wouldn't have married her without it, and she must have known it.

It was time to quit fucking crying over a girl that probably never even loved me anyway. *Had I ever loved her, though?*

No, was the honest answer to that question.

I *was* better off without her. Gray was right. I didn't miss Cassidy as much as I was furious about how she'd left me standing at the proverbial altar with my dick hanging out and thirty thousand dollars of non-refundable wedding cancellations. The blow to my ego in being dumped still stung, but I'd have to get over my butt hurt with that. I hadn't loved her any more than she'd loved me. Honestly, I doubted I'd ever fall in love. Maybe I was broken when it came to loving someone.

Sometimes we all needed a sharp kick in the balls to move on, I thought as the water came into view. Taking my own sharp kick from the waves would do me the most good. And then? *Forget the bitch, pay the debts, and move the fuck on with my life.*

Luckily, I'd been prepared when I'd met Gray at Jazz Street by wearing board shorts to our late lunch and taking my surfboard with me. As close a friend as Gray was, instinct had told me that our meal wouldn't go well. Probably because every time I met up with anyone these days, my failed wedding disaster cast an impossible-to-escape shadow over it.

It cast a shadow over my thoughts these days, too. By now, thanks to Cassidy, I knew more about the dark side of women than I cared to.

Ah yes, *women.*

Why did we chase after them? Barely memorable sex? I couldn't remember the last time my cock had been in her mouth for longer than two seconds. Or the cordial treatment in public that was probably all an act in the first place. Her BFF girlfriends tittering as they shopped away our joint finances, in on the big bad secret—that they didn't need us as much as we needed them. *Lies.* This was all a bored game for them, a hopeless clash of make-believe with reality. And, in the end, everyone lost. Their Disney Princess bubble view of men was burst, as was our hope for any companionship or comfort. I'd seen them, the longtime "tamed" husbands with the already-dead eyes. The last thing I wanted was to become one. She was right. *I'm not husband material, and I never fucking will be.* But she might also be wrong about the "being alone forever" thing. Wasn't it possible to have enough in a long-term relationship to keep me from being alone?

Once I finally arrived at my house, I sat for a minute, taking a breath. Mental rants like this—against Cassidy and women in general—were happening more often than I'd like. It wasn't good for me. Maybe *I* needed to go on a vacation somewhere…Costa Rica, Bermuda…somewhere hot and sleepy where I could drink away my problems for a good week or three on a beach with some waves.

Going on vacation right now wasn't an option with work. No, the closest thing I had to an escape was surfing, and I took it every chance I got.

I made a beeline for my house, tossed my shirt and shoes inside, tucked my beloved Hypto Krypto under my arm, and I was good to go.

Sinking my toes in the warm sand, my eyes closed with gratification.

Yes.

No matter what had happened before, things were going to be okay now. The ocean sent a beckoning finger of sea air up my nostrils. My eyes snapped open.

It's time.

Since it was the middle of a Wednesday

afternoon, the beach was empty—just how I liked it. Perfect for how I surfed.

Being out there alone with no one to be seen for miles made me feel like a king, one who tempted fate. Like a fearless explorer or adventurer. I'd loved Indiana Jones as a kid, and riding waves, which were as untamed a beast as Mother Nature gave us, was the closest I could get to my own modern-day adventure.

Sucking in a deep breath, I strode into the water.

Unhalting. The very best way to bear the uncomfortable cold shock of the water.

As it mercilessly encased my legs in its icy tendrils, I soldiered ahead. This was how you dealt with the cold, literally and figuratively. The same way I'd been dealing with the separation. One day after the next, hurling myself into work with a more determined, single-minded drive than I'd ever had.

Once the waves reached my waist, I clambered onto my board and started paddling to the approaching swells.

And then suddenly, I was there. As I was lifted, I arched my back, hyper-focused on popping up. This was it. If I wasn't focused, the unsympathetic wave's strength would slam me back down, mocking my paltry attempt.

My squint of focus relaxed only slightly with the realization that I'd done it. I was riding the sea.

Not conquering it, but moving with it—in a synchronized dance between wave and man. Saltwater hung from my face and a far-off gull cry echoed in my ears, and yet none of it mattered in this, this single, perfect instant when I was immortal. When the mirage of life opened its shaded doors to me.

And then the wave crashed, and I was freed, spewed out, to chase the next one. The next fleeting escape.

The next hour was more of the same. The wash of water over my eyes and ears. The dives, the falls, the bravery. My head resting on my board. My feet held fast on my board, sailing on pure liquid rush. The closest I could get to walking on water.

And then it was over.

But my mind was the textbook definition of *clear*. Maybe even *holy* calm had been achieved. Like the waves and the daring of them had somehow sloshed the disturbing thoughts out of my head.

No, there was only life, plain and simple and right. The cool lick of the water stroked my front, slipping down my body. The far-off wheeling seagulls, celebrating. The sweeping expanse of tan beach. Empty.

Almost.

Except her.

A girl who was…beautiful and carefree…

standing on the beach with the wind fluttering her sea-colored dress against her body and whipping her long dark-blonde hair across her face. She also looked straight at me as I came in from the water.

Or did she?

I craned my head over my shoulder, transported back to high school. One of the handful of times a hot girl—like Nina with her unsettling Spanish eyes, or Chelsey with her rainbow bracelets encircling each arm, or Jeanne with her tall boots on long lovely legs—waved at me, and I'd craned my head around my shoulder to confirm whether they were actually waving at me and not another uniformed boy with floppy hair in the mass of students.

But this time, there was no one and nothing else in sight except for an orange buoy bobbing innocuously in the sea. Only…me.

Catching my eye, a radiant smile emerged on the girl's face. She waved.

I guess that was a *yes?*

She *was* waving at me.

CHAPTER 2

"How are you liking it?" Stupid thing to ask, but my mouth seemed to be in the mood for *only* doing stupid with her, so I just went with it.

Her delicate fingers had formed a visor shading her from the sun as she peered up at me from where she was now sitting in the sand. "How am I liking what?"

Blankly, I stared at her. Really, I'd meant the beach. But now that I saw she had an open notebook in her lap and a sharpened pencil in her hand, I wanted to know what the half-visible image on the paper was. And she clearly had an accent—French maybe—which for some reason made me want to get to know her even more.

I gestured at her notebook. "How are you liking whatever you're doing?"

She bit her lip into a grin, glancing down.

When she aimed her dark eyes at me again, they carried the same radiance as her smile. "I love it."

I stood there awkwardly for a minute, debating whether to press her when it was obvious she was sidestepping my question.

With a half-smile and a toss of her head, she flicked her notebook to me, paper-side out. Striding forward and crouching down, I made out the drawing. A well-rendered sketch of Folly Beach showcasing some pumping waves and, what looked to be a small figure on a board.

"Sorry." She turned the drawing back around. "I have been at this for ages, but still get self-conscious. Some people despise being drawn."

Her pretty eyes flicked to me again, looking for some kind of a response.

I shrugged. "I'm only the size of a paper clip in your sketch." As her cheeks colored, a tempting thought occurred to me. And again, my mouth took over speaking more stupid shit I couldn't take back. "Actually, I've never had my portrait done. It could be cool. I mean, I could sit here for you with my board…if you want." *Your fucking mouth, dude.*

She paused, her gaze drifting away from me as she followed the undulating waves. Perhaps she sensed my innocent question was not all that innocent. I could see now that her blue dress was fishnet, with holes large enough for me to see the yellow bikini she wore underneath it. Plenty of her very lovely golden skin was visible too. I could sit and stare at her for a long time without getting bored. My view was certainly spectacular, and if she talked to me in that accent of hers while she drew, I'd like it even better.

She surprised me though when she gave me a vigorous nod. "As long as you are fine with sitting for a long time. An hour at the very most least."

The adorable double negative she added to the end of her sentence was the clincher for me…if I hadn't already been convinced. I slung my board down and sat beside it. "I've got time." *And for some reason, for her, I do have time.* It was as thought I'd slipped into an alternate reality. When had I ever answered, *I've got time?*

Something I couldn't name drew me to this girl. I wasn't able to walk away. My feet would simply not fucking move even as my brain shouted for them to go. Because I needed to find out who she was. Why was she here? Where did she live? I needed to know so much more about this beautiful exotic girl with the Parisian lilt to her words and the sexy smile, who wanted to draw my portrait.

Oh, yes.

She stood abruptly. "In that case it would be better if we sit in the shade. I was only sitting here because it was the only place with a good view of the water."

I swallowed back my grin at the purring quality of her "*r*"s, and got to my feet, gesturing with my hand. "There's a palm tree about a five-minute walk down that way. I'm Gage, by the way, and I live in that house over there." I pointed out my place for her, so she would feel—

Feel what? Safer? Assured I wasn't a serial killer? I had no fucking idea what I was even doing with this girl. Offering myself as a sketch model for a stranger—because she waved at me on the beach? Sounded fucking dumb when I spelled it out in my head. But that's exactly what I'd done. Happily, too.

Another brilliant smile lit up her face. "Gage, it is lovely to meet you. I am Giselle. Your plan is perfect."

Perfect all right. And I fucking love your name.

Five minutes later, my ass was planted in the sand with my surfboard across my knees and the mysterious Giselle studying me in silence.

She ripped a piece of paper out of her sketchpad and placed it on top. Feeling oddly self-conscious, I scratched at the side of my neck and wondered if I was going to regret this. "Am I allowed to talk?"

She fired back with a quick and firm, "No."

The disappointment must have showed on my face, because she laughed. "Of course, it is permitted." She then added a playful pat to my hand.

My dick twitched in my shorts and my hand tingled from her fingers, as I sat there and said…nothing. My brain needed to catch up— fucking quickly. This kind of shit did not happen to me. Pretty girls rendering me speechless with a simple touch to my hand and a few smiles? Not part of *my* universe. Could she be an alien female perhaps?

Biting her lip and brushing a stray curl out of her face, she said, "In actual fact, it is probably quite a lot better if you do talk."

"Great."

It occurred to me that I had absolutely no idea what to say to her. Everything seemed hopelessly stupid and trite. So, I settled on the most hopelessly stupid and trite question of all. "You're not from here, are you?"

Another laugh.

She'd started on the actual sketching, and since it involved her coffee-colored eyes bowed to her work instead of inspecting every inch of me, my shoulders relaxed a little.

"What gave me away?"

I bit back "everything" and instead settled on,

"Your dress."

In a roundabout way, it was true. The style was way more bohemian and less buttoned-down than Charleston's usual beach-chic locals or its beach-casual tourists.

She ran a hand over the fishnet material absently. "This dress I actually made myself." She smiled, drawing her arm down her body as if painting the picture of what she was saying. "Originally, when I saw this crazy too-large jumpsuit in the thrift shop, it looked so horrendous that I classed it as a lost cause. But something about the crochet fabric beckoned to me, so I bought it on a whim and decided to see what I could do with it."

My eyes spanned the dress, but even more so what was underneath the dress, trying to imagine how the gorgeous result in front of me could've ever looked horrendous.

"The material is very soft. Here, touch."

She offered the hem of her dress. It felt kind of stiff and rough to me rather than soft, but I didn't want to sound rude. I hoped she was so entranced in her drawing, she couldn't see my reaction at exactly how un-soft her blue crochet dress felt.

I caught her eyes sneaking my way before I clued in she was teasing me *again*. "Nice one," I said with a shake of my head.

Pausing, she clapped her hands together as more laughter poured out. "Ah, sorry. I really ought to stop. It's just that everyone here is so polite, I can't help but to tease."

Since I couldn't decide whether to be annoyed or intrigued, I settled on an easy laugh instead. "That's Charleston for you. Full of people who are polite to a fault."

She focused on her notebook again, her pencil scrabbling away. "And you?"

Her question caught me off guard, because I didn't want to talk about myself at all, but I couldn't deny her even the most basic of requests.

"And me, what?" I asked, even though I knew what she wanted to know.

Her eyes lifted momentarily from the sketch. "Are you like that too?"

The hardened patch of sand where I was sitting started to dig into my ass.

"It just helps," she explained. "For the portrait. I find knowing details about the sitter makes it easier to draw them. A more accurate portrayal, I guess."

Her words reminded me of what I'd heard about how artists developed not just an eye for detail, but for people too. For seeing beneath the façade and finding the truth the faces might tell.

"Doesn't your artist's eye tell you?" My question came out harsher than I intended.

Another smile twitched at the corner of her

mouth as she bit her bottom lip. "Yeah...so I think you are not."

"Polite to a fault? Unfortunately, not. It's why I don't always get by so well here."

"Then why do you stay?"

I shrugged. "It's home. It's all I know. I've travelled, sure, but I've never really felt like I belonged anywhere else."

"But you don't feel like you belong here either."

A few beats of awkward silence. Then, seeming to believe she'd said something she shouldn't have, she bit her lip again and said, "Sorry."

"Don't be sorry."

Right now, Giselle's words were like addicting stabs. I wanted to see how deep they could cut me before I bled.

"Tell me. Look and tell me. Tell me what you see."

The startling intensity of her eyes made me almost want to avert my gaze. But looking iris-deep into them, I'd swear they weren't just the melted-chocolate color I'd noticed at first, but layers upon layers of browns, sparkling with passion that stirred me up and put fear into me at the same time.

"Tell me," I urged, her silent stance suggesting she was considering it. "I can handle it, Giselle."

Once again, our eyes met, and a shock of

electric sensation zapped right through me.

She shook her head. "I don't know. It's better when I don't only look, but also"—her head tipped down—"touch too."

My cock heard her again, too, although I did my best to stifle it. The last thing I needed right now was to be flashing an erection while she had her attention fixed on me so diligently.

"That's fine," I told her.

She nodded, her eyes closing as her hands neared my face. Her fingertips gently slid up to my eyelids.

"Eyes closed for you too, Gage. It is easier."

I closed my eyes. Her hands started out on the rigid plane of my forehead, feeling out the strong brow bone my dad always used to boast about. Then they swept down, over my eyebrows. "You are a hard man. Closed off," she said softly, without a trace of judgment.

Cassidy said the same thing.

Even though I'd heard it *many* times before, coming from Giselle it didn't have the same sting.

Her hands swept down to my cheekbones.

"Proud."

My faults were being revealed one by one underneath her busy fingers. Why couldn't she spot anything good? This subconscious bullshit was probably only revealing the many negatives she guessed about me. By now, Giselle probably had me pegged as a cocky, unfeeling, rich boy who wasn't interested in anything more than getting laid.

It's true though.

When her fingers swept down around my eyes, however, she paused. "Sad." The word came out, softly, a little unwillingly.

My eyes snapped open as I ripped my face away from her hands.

Giselle blinked at me, as if startled from a deep trance. Her cheeks were now beet red.

"Sorry," she said again.

I shook my head, stretched out my arms, and rubbed at my temples. "You don't have to keep apologizing. I asked you to tell me. I was just…getting uncomfortable being in one position for so long."

Lame.

She nodded wordlessly, clearly seeing right through my obvious lie. But was it enough to have her make an excuse and leave my pathetic ass on the beach?

I didn't want her to leave, though.

"I'm sorry." I'd said those two words to Cassidy countless times but they sounded foreign on my lips when saying them to her. "I'm just not used to—"

"People just saying what they think?"

Another soft smile from her had me studying the sand where her toes were buried, the soft grains partially obscuring her feet at the end of her long lovely legs. "Yeah. It's a bit disarming…but I don't want you to stop doing it."

"Oh." Her lips formed an *O* in surprise. "And…you also wish for me to keep on drawing you?" She blushed as she asked the question.

"Yes. Please."

The next few minutes, she worked in concentrated silence. Although I was itching to talk to her, I kept quiet, figuring I'd blabbed enough already. But when she lifted a hand to twirl a strand of hair absently, revealing a vibrant wrist tattoo, I couldn't resist.

"What's that?"

She glanced down. "Oh, this?" Smiling, she lifted her wrist, so it was inches away from my face.

Many shades of color: azures, amethysts and every hue in between, expertly twined together into what looked to be a tiny sparrow. "I guess it is my spirit animal, you could say."

Above the colorful bird was the sweeping script of an *N*, and then below an *F*.

"Those letters, are they a French form of the compass?"

Giselle withdrew her wrist to hold it close to her. "My French accent is that much of a giveaway, yes?" she asked after a minute, with a little smile.

I nodded. She didn't say anything, though, and got back to her sketching. Apparently Giselle was the only one who got to dig deep.

"Do the letters stand for 'never fear'?"

As she glanced up, I caught the beginnings of a smile and then...sadness. I kept my gaze steady and determined, though. So far, Giselle had been the one leading and guiding our conversation. Now it was my turn.

"You are close. It's for 'never forget,'" she said after a minute, her eyes growing more distant.

As if sensing my next question, she explained, "It is reminder. For why I left home. Why I came here."

By now, she looked so distraught that I only wanted to take her in my arms and comfort her. Instead, frustration thrummed in me—at myself, for prying where I shouldn't have.

"Listen, Giselle..." I took her hand. "I—"

And then, a gust of wind snatched her drawing away. As it sailed through the air, Giselle leapt up, taking off after it. "Merde!"

I scrambled up and after her, already several paces behind. Suddenly, with a cry, Giselle toppled to the sand.

When I reached her, her foot was clasped in her hands and her toe was streaming blood.

"Shit. Are you all right?"

Giselle shot a glare at the nearby rock jutting up from the sand responsible for her injury. Then, she tossed a wistful look over her shoulder as the wind whisked the paper out of sight. "Looks like that is the end of your portrait, Gage."

Her jaw set in pain, as I looked around for something to wrap her toe in. The best option was a piece of palm leaf from the nearby tree. She barely made a noise while I fiddled with the leaf. Cassidy would have been crying blue murder, demanding to sue the beach for a hidden rock. Although, she'd never allow sand to get between her manicured toes, so I guessed that point was moot. Yet, Giselle was quiet. *Fearless.* I tied the leaf around her foot twice, but despite the way I bound it, red blood still seeped through my makeshift bandage. *Should I take her to my place for some proper first aid?*

She gave a small, bitter laugh. "Ought to have been more careful. I am one for the mishaps. And then there is the whole name of this beach."

Despite the situation, I found myself smirking. "Folly Beach, yeah."

I made up my mind.

Before I could think about it, I grabbed my surfboard and swept her up in my arms. There was a second or two of a communal balancing act—but she ended up higher in my arms, and my Hypto Krypto in hers. It would work.

"What are you doing?"

"Taking you to my house. The hospital is a good thirty minutes away, and even if you just want to go to a drugstore, that's a twenty-minute walk. My house is about five."

Giselle relaxed in my arms. "All righty then." She peeled her eyes away from the reds and pinks the setting sun was flinging into the sky and aimed a testy look up to me. "Promise me you are not an absurdly attractive axe murderer?" *Absurdly attractive axe murderer? Where have you come from, Giselle?*

I gave her a small squeeze. "Promise."

Our eyes locked together.

Adrenaline flowed through my veins as we returned to her notebook underneath the palm tree. We gathered up everything a second time between us, and I carried her to my beach house.

Except this time as I walked, "*absurdly attractive* axe murderer" ran through my head like an addictive sort of tongue twister.

And she is an alluring, French beach fairy.

CHAPTER 3

"So, we have pink, blue, or regular old white."

At the kitchen table with her injured foot propped up on a dinner plate, Giselle tilted her head at me quizzically.

"Bandages," I said, holding up the three cloths.

I left it at that. I wasn't going to explain how my ex was the reason I had pink and blue cloth bandages in the first aid kit. She was a smart girl, and probably already had it figured out anyway in the time it took me throw on jeans and T-shirt. Even though I loathed the feel of salty skin under clothes, I'd shower later. Right now, I had a beautiful woman in pain to tend to. She crinkled her nose at me and said, "What the hell, I choose pink."

Fuckin' adorable.

After inspecting and cleaning her cut, the injury didn't look quite as bad as I'd originally thought, so a simple wrapping over some antibacterial would probably best do the job. If her toe was broken, then time was the only thing to heal it. Thankfully it wasn't her big toe that had taken the blow against the rock. I could feel her eyes on me as I worked, so I looked up and gave *her* a smile. She'd given me so many. *Smiles.* In a short time, I'd become rather addicted to Giselle's smiles. I didn't have a lot of experience with smiling women—*any really*—but I knew enough to understand that I liked them from her. A whole fucking lot.

"What?" she asked.

"Your English." I made the final wrap-around before tucking the excess pink fabric in. "How'd you learn to speak English so well?"

"Oh that," she said sweeping out her hand. "I was just a nerd, I suppose. Ever since I was small, my dream was to see with my own eyes the America I'd read about in my textbooks and seen in the movies. The America with the mint-green goddess of Liberty, the delicious apple pie, and where everyone was so loud and wild and *raw*. So, in class I was one of the few ones who paid attention and studied on my own. And so"—she cracked a smile—"here I am."

"Is it what you expected?"

Her head shake was decisive. "Nope."

But that still hadn't told me what I really wanted to know. "Why here, though? Charleston, hell—or even South Carolina for that matter—isn't exactly on most foreign traveler's top ten."

"I already did check out New York City and Boston." She made a quick sequence of finger tapping, from her thumb to her pinky, as if that was how fast her trip had gone by. "Anyway, I ran out of money and was tired of all the city, city, cities. I wanted somewhere more quiet…on a beach. Like Cannes in France, but small."

"You choose well then. Guess your English lessons paid off."

Her eyes lit up with mischief. "Not exactly. Our English classes themselves were trash—all Disney movies, and mocking whatever the teacher said to us. It was more my stubborn pigheadedness, as my père used to say, that got me anywhere, and studying at home with Brynne, an American university student who lived with us in Paris. I did my lessons with her. Things like that."

I nodded. "The French classes at the private school I went to were pretty much trash too. I mean, don't get me wrong, the teachers really tried. But I think it's like you said, most of us kids just weren't interested. My French exam in the twelfth grade was passed by the slimmest of margins—sixty-one percent and only by writing *Dr. & Mrs. Vandertramp* on my frog eraser."

Giselle stuck out her bottom lip at me in a pout. "Alors tu ne peux pas parler à moi?"

My blank stare probably said it all, as my dismal years of primary French failed to comprehend what she'd said. "Uh, bonjour?"

Giselle threw her head back and laughed, the deep rumble making her body shake all the way from the long length of her dark golden hair down to her delicate tan feet. After few seconds, she paused. Sticking up the big pink mummified creation that was her middle toe, she wiggled it, and laughed some more. "It is like a big pink marshmallow."

"Just don't go eating it," I said wryly, seeing that she did have a point.

She stuck her tongue out at me playfully, and then it hit me. "Hey, you must be hungry. Sorry, I didn't even think to ask."

Giselle nodded her head up and down dramatically. "The *worst* host, you are."

Her frown held for a quarter of a second before it cracked, letting loose another peal of laughter. "Although I would appreciate anything you have, really." Her smile sheepish, she added, "When I get into drawing like I do, I often forget to eat."

I strode over to the pantry and then looked back over at her. "I don't know. I feel like I really have to live up to this worst host thing." I wasn't one to tease in conversation, but with her it felt very natural. *Easy.*

Our eyes locked on to each other's in a sort of sarcastic staring contest. *What were we even doing here?*

Crossing her arms across her chest, Giselle flicked her head in a sideways uncaring motion. "At least when I die of starvation, you will not have to waste any more of your beloved pink bandages on my corpse."

Opening the cupboard, I retrieved a package and tossed it at her. "That should hold off your starvation for at least another hour or two."

She caught the bag of giant marshmallows and set it on the table with a grin. "My subconscious powers of suggestion worked."

I nodded, sitting at the table. "You're lucky you didn't say your bandage looked like a mushroom, because I have some of those too."

She wrinkled her nose adorably.

I noticed our feet were touching under the table. Giselle's good foot had draped lazily down and was now resting against mine. She didn't try to move it either, as she busied herself with trying to open the bag of marshmallows.

Frustrated, she shoved the bag over to me. "If you meant to mock me by providing me with a marshmallow bag that doesn't open, congratulations, you have succeeded."

With one quick rip I tore open the bag and tossed a marshmallow her way.

Giselle jerked toward it and caught the marshmallow neatly in her mouth.

Impressive.

As she chewed, she winked at me, with what was most certainly a surprised expression on my face. "Drawing is not my only skill."

"That's obvious." Her words sent a stroke of excitement down to my cock, keeping me on the edge. Just being around this unexpected woman, I sensed there was more truth to her words than even she herself realized. What would it be like to be where that marshmallow was right now...pressed against her rosy lips? Having her tongue moving against me...laving and sucking. *Shit.*

Something soft hit the side of my face. Giselle's expression of pure innocence changed to disbelieving when I picked up the marshmallow she'd thrown and tossed the entire thing in my mouth.

"How?"

As her brown eyes widened, I managed to squeeze another giant one into my mouth and kept on chewing.

As she raised her half-eaten marshmallow and pointed at my mouth expectantly, I shook my head and mumbled, "Hink hat's it."

Lips pursed, Giselle leaned over, steadying herself on the table with the hand that wasn't clasping her own half of a marshmallow.

Determined, she mashed her marshmallow half into my already stuffed mouth slowly. The whole process was as sexy as fuck, and I did not stop her. *Couldn't*. Once finished, she clapped her hands together. "Ha!"

Her eyes dipped to my lips, paused. Our eyes met and held. Every atom in me urged me to lunge forward and press my marshmallow-coated lips to hers.

But I didn't.

I got up from my chair instead and strode over to the sink, cranked on the faucet, and shoved my hands under the cold stream. This was not for the purpose of cleaning my sticky fingers or mouth, but actually to force myself into some space and perspective.

I'd just met this girl, and she was clearly in a vulnerable situation with an injured foot. Whatever my simmering mental state, right now wasn't the time to act upon my urges with a total stranger.

But right now I *did have* Giselle sitting at my kitchen table, with her features set into what looked to be pain.

"You okay?" I asked.

She mustered up an unconvincing smile. "I will

live."

I felt a bit helpless, and it was fucking frustrating seeing her this way. "In France, what do they do for pain? Like, to take your mind off it?"

A smile lit in her eyes. "The same way I presume they do here in America."

I liked the sound of this already. "Oh?"

She glanced down, her cheeks blushing pink. "Wine."

She looked back at me, meeting my gaze brazenly this time. For what seemed like one long dreamlike minute, we stared at each other. Was it just my imagination? Or did Giselle have more than a fair idea of what I'd like to do with her? Maybe something she wanted…too.

She was the first to tear her eyes away. "Sorry. That was a bit assuming of me, asking for wine after you have been so generous and accommodating already. You do not have to. In fact, forget about it."

I'd already made my way to the wine cupboard, though. "You don't have to apologize for anything. Before I met you, I'd had a shit day myself. Some wine would be an excellent way to top off the night. I'll even throw in cheese and crackers while I'm at it to show you my social skills are not a complete waste of—"

As soon as the words were out of my mouth, I realized I couldn't just toss her out onto the beach when we were finished drinking the wine. She didn't have a car or a way to get home that I knew of, and she wasn't walking back in the dark with an injured foot.

"Would you like me to drive you where you're staying?"

She shook her head no.

"Sorry, I didn't even ask you about that before I brought you here. I forgot—I don't even know where you live." My rambling seemed to do nothing in the way of earning me any more information from her, so I finished it by making her an offer. "Although, you're more than welcome to stay here too, if you'd prefer." *Oh, that's smart, asshole.*

Yet I really wanted her to say yes. *What the fuck, man.*

Giselle looked past me. "Whatever is easiest for you is perfect for me."

My decision was big, significant—and yet I made it in a split-second, sensing that if I pondered for a second longer then I wouldn't firm up the offer. I didn't invite women to my house to stay the night. Ever. Not even pre-Cassidy.

"Then you can stay. But I only have one bedroom furnished at the moment, so I'll sleep on the couch."

At this, Giselle firmly shook her head no. "It would be impossible for me to stay if you did that.

Please, let me have the couch. These past few months I have slept on the odd couch for a night or two when necessary, and in horribly crummy hostile beds that are like glorified sacks of potatoes."

I tried to bite back my grin...and failed.

"What is so amusing to you, Gage?"

You. Everything you say. The way you are.

"Just, the beds. Did you mean *hostel* beds, or were the beds themselves actually *hostile* to you?"

Hearing her mistake, Giselle giggled while I scanned the bottles in the wine case carefully. "How does *Château Margaux 2010* sound?"

Giselle clapped a hand to her lips. "Oh no, I could never. That wine is...rare and very expensive."

She was right...and knowledgeable about wine. Cassidy's parents had gifted us the bottle. A thousand-dollar bottle of cabernet to enjoy on our honeymoon. In the madness of the wedding cancellation and shipping out Cassidy's things, I'd forgotten about it. And nobody had asked for it back, so they'd probably thought it was tainted from its original purpose. Good thing I didn't share their sentiments.

I set it on the marble countertop and popped the cork, pouring two glasses and then handing her one. "I think you can, Giselle. Enjoy it while I set up the rest of our night-time feast."

Smiling slightly, she accepted her glass without a

word.

When I returned with the cheese and crackers, I didn't miss her wince of pain as she got up and tried to follow me. I glanced to the adjoined living room. "Here, let's get you on the couch now."

She made no protest as I swept her up again and carried her over, although she did let out a small exhale of surprise. "You made that look very simple."

That's because it is. I set her down on the suede cushions, grinning like an idiot. "I'm sure if you went to the gym as much as I do…plus, you are easy to carry." *I've never carried a woman like this. For some insane reason, it felt right. She felt right in my arms.*

"Ha." Giselle threw up a hand. "Do not lie."

"I'm not lying," I said, passing her glass to her and depositing myself on the opposite end of the couch.

I was far enough away that when she lifted her glass to make a toast, I had to really reach in order to clink my glass to hers. "To a failed drawing, but a successful evening nonetheless, yes?" she said.

I nodded slowly and tasted my wine. We stared at each other, shared shy smiles, and mostly said nothing. Right now, in the warm, dim lights of my living room, she was all I could see. In her blue dress, with her golden skin and long silky hair—a contrast to the soft tone of my sofa—she looked…beautiful. *Perfect.* Like there was nothing else in the room to look at but her. It took all of my self-control not to kiss her.

So, we sipped and ate in a comfortable silence instead. As the clock ticked out the minutes, I pushed away a hundred different comments and excuses to talk to her, because sitting beside her like this was amazing. Not in any way awkward. Giselle was simply easy to be with, and I didn't want the moment to end.

"Gage?"

"Yes?"

Seeing her glass was empty, I reached for the bottle to refill her glass, but she declined with a sad smile.

"This has been more than enough. It has been months, to tell you the truth. I-I..." She shook her head, and another sad smile appeared on her lovely face. "No matter. The point is"—she met my eyes and bit on her luscious bottom lip again—"I really just want to thank you...for your incredible kindness today."

I tried to keep my focus on her eyes and not the distracting lip-biting thing she did so well. "Of course." Right this second, every part of me was screaming to move closer to her, to meet those lips of hers that looked so delicious.

Instead, I got up from the sofa and made my way to the kitchen with the cheese plate and the half-empty bottle. "Tomorrow, I've got an early morning. Should probably be getting to bed." It was a lie, though. *You're a pussy.*

But what the hell was I supposed to do? Giselle was essentially a stranger. She probably didn't want some horny American guy leering at her. Let along touching her. *Kissing her. Tasting her.*

Oh fuck. *Yeah, you're still a pussy.*

"Oh. Of course," she said, her tone quiet, unassuming…possibly disappointed even. I refused to look her way. The next words she spoke to me were dismissive, coming from a stranger's voice. "You may turn off the light on your way up."

No.

Frustration rattled through me as I snapped off the light switch. I was halfway to the staircase when she said, "And Gage?"

"Yeah?"

"Can you come back for a moment? There is just one more thing I want to say to you."

Caution had every hair on my body standing on end, but now that my feet had been given permission to do what they'd been itching to for hours, they strode back to her obediently.

As I stood behind the couch and she peered up at me, I came to another realization. In the moonlight, her features had assumed an almost mystical clarity, as if this were her intended state all along. Like she was always meant to be here in my house, on my sofa, staring up at me, wanting me to be with her. There couldn't be any other reason.

"Closer," her whisper commanded. So, I dipped my head down slightly, allowing the last of my good sense to give the fuck up in defeat.

She beckoned me again, and again I leaned in closer.

And even closer still, until any kind of retreat had become a ridiculous impossibility.

As her luscious lips swept up to mine, in the instant before they met, she murmured, "I want to kiss you good night."

CHAPTER 4

Her lips against mine were the absolute end of it. The end of my self-control. The end of dancing around the intense attraction we both felt. One movement followed another, all joined in a matrix of predictability.

The initial soft crush of her lips to mine doomed me. Without a trace of uncertainty, Giselle knew what she was doing, and what she wanted. She wanted me. I wanted her too, but it was more a realization on my part that our first kiss changed something *inside* me. I couldn't explain it, but I certainly felt whatever *it* was, wrapping around me, growing and building as our lips moved together.

Her tongue dove in to tease with mine, darting in and out of my mouth, leading me on a wild chase that only ramped me up more.

By the time I'd clambered onto the couch with her, our hands were all over each other as if we both already knew the landscape. Although her crochet dress seemed impossibly hole-filled, and my fingertips kept getting snagged in the threads as I stroked over her beautiful body. If it bothered Giselle, she didn't let on. Her own hands were dipping underneath my shirt to sear into my skin. We both pushed, sought to be closer. Needed our skin to be touching.

I whipped my shirt over my head and tossed it. With that useless obstruction gone, her palms pressed along the contours of my chest as if she were a sculptor hand-fashioning her creation—molding the clay to her will—and I was her clay. *Willingly.*

I let her touch me. I would have done anything she wanted from me in this moment. In the pale darkness, my hands spanned her breasts over the dress. God, I wanted it all off so I could see her in the moonlight. I didn't ask. I sat her up and swept the dress over her head without a word.

Silent, sexy Giselle was apparently in agreement with me, because as soon as the dress was off her body she brought her hands to the back of her neck…and pulled on the tie that held the top of her bathing suit up. The two yellow halves separated as gravity took over and revealed the most magnificent tits I'd ever seen…or imagined. *Fucking gorgeous.*

Two gloriously full mounds with dark pink nipples tightened into buds. When I cupped them, she shivered...or maybe that was me. They felt exquisitely soft, and in desperate need of being kissed and sucked and licked.

As my lips dipped to those awaiting nipples, I heard the words that made my already rock-hard dick gunning to escape from my jeans. "Oh, *oui*."

I almost came.

Those two words from her did something to me.

With my lips sucking on her nipples, her fingertips found their way through my hair as we battled it out. She arched her back and moaned in French. Yes, she fucking did. Giselle's lovely moans and sighs and whimpers were clearly voiced to me in French...rather than English. This was something I understood as clearly as my name.

The pebbled bud of her nipple and the softness below felt so good in my mouth as I sucked on it, I didn't think I could pull away. I forced myself to move to the other side with a groan of my own. Closing my palm around the first breast, I tugged on the nipple while I sucked on her new one. I might be at this for hours. How would it be possible to get enough of her perfect, gorgeous tits?

As another shiver ripped through her—along with more whines in French—I knew I was doing what she liked. Her reactions to my kisses and touches did wonderful things for my ego. Seeing her in such a state of abandonment pushed me to ask for more.

My hands went to her sides and then down her long, lovely legs before pausing.

Her eyes fluttered open only for an instant, one brow cocked, as if asking me, *"What are you waiting for?"*

I didn't need to voice my answer, because my hands were already stroking the inside of her thighs and up and up…until they stopped at her bikini bottoms—a yellow frill of fabric that was wonderfully wet right where it should be.

Christ. She's not faking this. She's turned on. *Fuck*, yes. As we continued eye-fucking, my fingers explored. First, rubbing over the outside of the wet fabric covering her pussy, and enjoying the shudder that swept through her whole body. The eager part of me wanted to yank those yellow bottoms down her legs to see the full glory of her. But the other hungry part didn't want to pause for a second, didn't want any chance of slowing down, ruining this. No. It was too perfect right now. *She's too perfect to be real.*

As our lips twisted and my tongue claimed her mouth with a foreshadowing of what I'd be doing later with my cock below, I dared to dip my hand under the fabric to bury my fingers in her wet heat.

Giselle moaned decadently into my mouth.

I barely noticed my jeans being tugged, because

my fingers were busy sliding into her incredibly tight, warm pussy. As she clenched around my two fingers, I felt my jeans pushed down. Clearly Giselle's clever work, if the woozy smile on her lips was any indication.

I countered that by wrenching her bikini bottoms down to her feet. With one sweep of her foot, she propelled them through the air.

We followed the path with our eyes and saw where they landed with a soft swish onto my coffee table. Then we looked back at each other, and burst into laughter. For a fleeting second, it was almost as though things were innocent like before. Like this was our secret dream or fantasy nobody would ever know except for the two of us.

But then I looked at her—completely naked, *spectacular*, and ready to be fucked by me—and I was lost again. Her clever hands gripped the waistband of my briefs and dragged those fuckers down my legs. As my cock dipped up and Giselle's mouth formed an *O*, I knew something was different. I couldn't explain what I felt, but I recognized this experience as something new.

When the final barrier between was gone, our bodies collided into each other. Breasts to chest, lips to neck, hip to hip. Hands went everywhere. Long, golden hair became tangled in my fingers as I held her down and sucked on her tits again.

When my hard cock kissed in between her legs, my eyes snapped open at the same time hers did.

One look at those parted lips and heaving chest, and I knew it was time. "I have to get a condom. Don't move, gorgeous." I kissed her quickly on the lips and hauled myself off her. *Fucking worst torture ever.* Stumbling around in the dark for a condom took too long, but I finally managed to find one and roll it onto my aching cock.

She held both arms out to me in the sweetest welcome. As I eased myself on top of her, she adjusted for me, opening her legs to allow for the perfect fit of our bodies. I fell into another deeper kiss, but I couldn't quite shut my eyes. No, I needed to see the expression on her face when I first slid inside her.

I watched the head of my cock sink into her pretty pussy and kept going. As I penetrated her more deeply, her whole face slackened in pleasure. Her half-lidded eyes looked at me in urgent need.

Because it felt *So. Fucking. Good.* with her.

And with every one of my strokes, her whole body responded, thrumming with the same frenetic energy consuming me—almost as if her body couldn't bear a feeling this good or might burst from the impossible joy of it.

With every one of my thrusts she lifted and twisted to meet it. Every single slide into her depths was a new surge of ecstasy. My actions were less than conscious, urges acting out of their own accord, using our bodies for their purposes. And still, I couldn't close my eyes.

With hers still half open and her parted lips moaning sighs and gasping in French, she was into watching us fuck as I was.

Was out of my hands anyway. I couldn't take my eyes off her.

Normally, I'm seized with urgency while fucking. Throwing myself into one position after the next, trying to fulfill every desire as much as physically possible. But this time, with Giselle, *this* was enough. In and out. Farther and deeper and hotter. It felt like we were perfecting the act together. Like anything more, any subtle change would've taken away from the perfection. As if this intense physical connection was all we needed...*or would ever need.*.

Already, I felt like I was going to lose it. Clenching my teeth together, I focused control on holding off as long as possible; but when my thrusts became sharper and hungrier, when my pace rocketed to top level and the cries falling from her lips joined mine into one breathless call, I knew it was time to make her come.

My hands found her tits and squeezed as I drilled into her, urging her on and on and on...until she broke apart for me. She was beautiful as she came. Beautiful to feel, too. I felt her pussy begin to spasm and clutch at my cock so tightly it almost couldn't be real. Her whole body went rigid and then started to shake as her climax took her over. Magical words fell from her lips, "Oh, oui...oui...*oui!*"

Words, which became a perfect trigger for me,

sent my own orgasm crashing down with exquisite brutal intensity right behind hers. As I emptied into her, she thrashed and arched against me—the beautiful wildness of her body in the throes of passion something I never wanted to forget. I *wouldn't* ever forget this moment with her.

And then, all there was left to do was hold and kiss her until the aftershocks faded and we could breathe again. I managed to ditch the condom and settle us under the afghan I pulled from the back of the couch. I drew her close and breathed in the sweetness of her perfume mixed with the unmistakable scent of amazing and superb fucking. *Intense, exceptional, unsurpassed fucking.*

Our arms and legs were tangled together peacefully when the warm blanket of sleep finally settled over me.

CHAPTER 5

I woke up alone in my quiet house.

Sitting straight up, I rubbed my eyes and studied my surroundings. The fact I'd slept naked on the couch confirmed that the wild romp with Giselle last night actually *had* happened.

I called her name.

Silence.

I didn't see her yellow bikini or her blue dress anywhere either. Would she have gone without saying something? I didn't think so, but then I didn't really know anything about the woman I'd spent my night with, other than how amazing she'd felt in my arms while I was inside her. I didn't even know her last fucking name let alone her number.

I grabbed my jeans from the floor, pulled them on...and went searching, chastising myself the whole way.

You met a pretty French artist and lost your shit completely.

Yep. Pretty much that.

I'd only known her one meager day. My anticipation of seeing her again was probably just the aftereffect of how great the sex had been.

I told myself that as I stormed through my house searching for her. The only visible trace that she'd been here was the bag of marshmallows on the table and the two empty wineglasses by the sink.

Heading outside, I scanned up and down the beach, hoping she might be sketching another picture from the sand.

She wasn't.

Giselle was gone, and she'd left me with absolutely no way to reach her.

Fuck.

I RETRACED MY STEPS with her from yesterday in an attempt to dislodge the growing certainty that Giselle really had just up and left after our amazing night together.

I spent the next hours in a determined blur trying to find her. That my French friend had really left without saying goodbye didn't seem possible. I felt sort of locked in motion; threading my way from one unlikely spot to another, figuring eventually that I'd find her at one of them.

I stopped by the nearby BLU restaurant, the Surf Bar, then back to the house, then drove into town to do the rounds. I hit up the usual public places. The Main County Public Library. The City Market. Even freaking *D'Alessandro's Pizza*. And at every single one of them, it was the same story.

"Long dark blonde hair and wearing a blue crochet dress? Nope, haven't seeing her. Why do you ask?"

Each time the question was asked by well-meaning but nosy friends of friends, it took all of my tact to sidestep their question with a polite waved "thanks", and leave it at that. No way was I in the mood to come up with some clever lie.

By lunchtime, though, I was defeated. And hungry as hell.

At Bohemian Bull, while devouring a charbroiled chicken burger, I answered my phone.

"Want to go surfing?"

Reid, sounding as cheery as I was not.

"Now?" I asked, glancing outside.

Okay, so it *was* sunny. But the prospect of actually *doing* work on this madcap Thursday felt like being woken up from a drowning dream.

"No, I was thinking more like in 2022," Reid said. "Yes now, Gage. In thirty minutes, if you want. Meet me on the beach."

I paused. My profoundly shitty mood would be drastically improved by surfing. Although I didn't exactly relish being around anyone else right now, with my wound still fresh from the morning.

"You still pissed about the Lena thing?" Reid asked.

"Yeah," I said noncommittally. "But I'll see you on the beach in thirty."

I DROVE BACK TO THE HOUSE, picked up my board, and was on the beach quickly enough. Reid was already hitting the waves. A few minutes later, I was out there with him.

Surfing with Reid was a distraction. The waves were hollow and peeling, but with such short intervals between sets there wasn't really time for actual conversation. Definitely what I needed, even though my head kept asking the same question. *Why the hell didn't she stick around?*

After our session, when we were walking back

onto the beach, I saw it.

Caught in the knots of a lilac bush, a familiar-looking piece of paper.

Reid said something to me, but I ignored him as I jogged to the paper, certain it wouldn't be what I hoped it was.

"Hey, kinda looks like you," Reid said from over my shoulder.

I nodded. Sketched in skillful lines, Giselle's portrait of me was a little ragged and smudged in places but still in one piece. *God, she's talented.* I wasn't sure how much I wanted to tell Reid, if anything at all.

My eyes stopped on the corner of the paper, which bore a distinctive embossed *E*. Where had I seen that before?

"Hell, it's been ages since I've been to Elysium," Reid said thoughtfully.

My questioning glance only made him shrug.

"You know, that fancy art shop downtown?"

Bingo. The façade of the store flashed in my mind. White Grecian-columned exterior, like it was a temple to the arts. An interior like a hippie's wet dream, with tie-dyed colors splayed everywhere. If that was where Giselle had gotten this paper from, that meant...

"Want to go there?" I asked abruptly.

Amusement taking over his face, Reid leaned on his board, which he had propped in the sand, and settled in for a good long wait as I looked at him— stone-faced.

I knew Reid well, and also what would get me off the hook with him. Clearly, this was going to require me dishing out some details.

"Some girl I met. We had a great time together and then got separated."

Reid dragged a hand through his wet hair before hoisting his board under his arm with another shrug.

"Sure, lover boy, we can go there."

Irritation sparked through me, but I followed him nonetheless. I wanted some company for this next part of my search. I wasn't sure why, other than a vague uneasiness I might benefit from some backup.

Uneasiness I was heading into some dangerous *uncharted* territory...for my heart.

ELYSIUM WAS JUST AS I REMEMBERED it. From its walls and floors painted in vibrant shades down to the now-ancient owner. The last time I'd been here was probably more than ten years ago, for some project at school. I recognized the grumbly old bat from back then and she seemed mostly unchanged.

"Revealing customer information is against the

law," she said with a toss of her frizzy white-haired head to my question about a girl matching Giselle's description. *As if that concoction of "herbs" I smell isn't, lady.*

She aimed her red-rimmed eyes at Reid and then me before turning away to rifle under the counter.

I looked to Reid for help as he muttered, "The shit I do…"

"Ma'am." He leaned on the desk.

She bobbed her head up and cocked a brow at him impatiently. "Really nice place you've got here. Decorated it yourself?"

With a frown set so deep into her face that I wondered if it would ever come out, she nodded warily.

Reid then glanced around the shop, taking it all in with a wistful sigh. "You made all of this with your husband, didn't you?"

Miraculously, the frowning set of wrinkles on her face softened. She *almost* smiled. "Took us months. We almost didn't think it would be ready in time. Didn't even know whether the store would work, but here it is still thriving all these years later."

Reid rubbed the side of his jaw like that was the most fascinating thing he'd heard all week. "It's obviously been in exceptional hands then. Kudos to you." Then, he gestured to me. "My friend Gage here, the person he's asking about, well, they have a connection. He's not some crazy creeper, I can attest to that. He's just a guy who's looking for a girl. There was this...misfortune...where they were separated without getting each other's information. So if you had her phone number that would do him a world of good."

The woman gave me a long, hard look before tapping a finger on the mouse connected to her ancient desktop. After a beat and a pause, she said, "Unlucky for you we don't deal with phone numbers. Phone calls aren't our style." My whole body sagged in defeat. *Fuck*.

"But"—Old Bat Art Lady lifted her eyes upward, as if seeking guidance from above—"*some people* set up accounts to have things delivered directly...like Giselle Fleury, 24 Clair Creek Lane." Clearly, she'd made her decision in advance because of what she said next. "Don't thank me for the information because I didn't tell you a thing. You only overhead my mention of the details of a client's delivery. In fact, don't say anything to me unless it's to ask for the price of whatever you're buying before you go." She had game, I'd give her that much. I also now had a way to find Giselle, so I didn't even care Old Bat Art Lady was grifting me.

Reid nodded gravely.

I followed her very specific instructions. "How much for three pads of this fine sketching paper, ma'am?"

She finally cracked the beginnings of a smile when she gave me the total for my purchase.

We waited until we were outside before the congratulatory knuckle tap. Then Reid stepped back and leaned on the wall of the store, that annoying debonair-Southern-gentleman act of his in full fuckin' swing and asked me the question.

"So, you want to tell me why you're stuck on this girl, Gage?"

I jostled the bag holding the three sketchpads I'd just bought for Giselle and shook my head.

"No. I'm not stuck on her. It's...only that we got separated...and I just want to make sure she's okay. She hurt her foot." *The truth—mostly.*

Reid nodded with the air of someone who didn't believe a word I'd said but would pretend to buy it for my sake anyway. Clapping his hand on my back, he said, "I'll leave you to it then. Take care of yourself, brother."

I gave him a shoulder bump. "You too. Thanks for wooing the info out of the crazy old bat for me. I owe you one."

After he left, it gradually dawned on me that our hasty victory wasn't exactly one. I hadn't gotten Giselle's phone number as I'd hoped. I'd gotten her *address*, which demanded a very different commitment—and potentially different interpretation by Giselle herself. Although she had seemed reckless and easygoing in some ways, what if she thought me

62

showing up at her place unannounced was super creepy and stalkerish?

Reading the address I'd recorded on my phone, I squared my shoulders. Although the normal way of getting Giselle's number and shooting her a call or a text would have been preferable, I didn't have that option. And it wasn't acceptable to not see her again. I felt something for her and wanted to explore...wanted to explore something. *Even though I had no clue if she feels anything for me.* It was either this or nothing.

Tucking my phone in my pocket, I set off for home. If worst came to worst, it would be the same as me doing nothing at all—and never seeing someone who brought unexpected light into my life again. *And that feels terribly wrong.*

I WAITED UNTIL THE NEXT MORNING.

It wasn't that far so I walked, mulling over my nonchalance about her to Reid, and feeling annoyed with myself. Why couldn't I have admitted that I'd had a great time with Giselle and wanted to see her again? What was the big deal?

Instinctively, I avoided answering my own question. Something told me I wouldn't like the answer. Already, the lengths I'd gone to see this French girl again was unsettling. I didn't pursue. I didn't put myself out unless it was for my business. *So, why her?*

A quick ten minutes later I was walking down Bluff Lane, grinning as I took in the pastel, low-lying structures. Of course Giselle would be staying on Rainbow Row. I should've guessed.

I'd made it to 10 Clair Creek when I saw her. Headed straight for me and looking just as beautiful as I remembered. *Because the memory of her is something permanent now.* She was wearing a short yellow dress instead of a blue one, but her long lovely legs looked just as gorgeous regardless of the color. *I had my cock buried between those lovely legs.* The frown she also wore once she recognized me didn't retract from her beauty. *Don't fuck this up. No matter what.*

"Giselle."

"Gage."

Her cheeks had a sun-kissed hue.

"I am—"

"I know I—"

Speaking at the same time, we broke off, laughing.

"I'm so sorry about yesterday," she said quickly. "When I woke up, you looked so deep in sleep, I would not allow myself to disturb you. It was better for me to go quietly…I felt I'd caused you enough trouble already."

I nodded, digesting her words. They made sense, although they still weren't exactly satisfying. "I understand I guess. I wanted to see you again, and I

64

was concerned about you leaving without telling me especially when you were hurt. I was worried about you." I looked at her foot, relieved to see my pink marshmallow bandage had been replaced with a discreet flesh-colored Band-Aid. Her toenails were now a similar pink though. Pretty feet...pretty girl. *So fuckin' pretty.* "How are you?"

The corner of her lips twitched into a smile. "Such a gentleman you are. And I thank you for asking about my poor toe. It is much improved today, thanks to you."

"I'm glad it's better today. Where are you going right now?" I couldn't resist asking, even though it was clear I was taking a liberty with her she'd not granted me yet.

"Ahh, yes well, I have an important meeting with my landlord right now. I...I cannot be late."

Like a school boy virgin, I blurted, "What would you say to going on a date with me later?"

The beginnings of her smile disappeared just as quickly. She shook her head sadly without looking at me.

"Unfortunately, that may not be a good idea."

"Why not?"

"Because...I have reasons."

I searched her face for answers I'd probably never find. But man, I wanted to know her reasons...so badly. Nearby birds chattered cheerily, far-off children squealed in either joy or rage, and something about Giselle's tense stance gave me pause.

It wasn't that she didn't want me here. It was that she *did*.

I shifted from one foot to another, weighing my options. Pushing her was not only bad manners, but potentially stupid. It could be that my attraction to Giselle was through a fool's rose-colored glasses. *But it isn't, and you fucking know it.*

"So, that's a no?" I asked.

She gave her head a single shake and then bit down on her bottom lip. "But it is not a *yes* either."

And, just like that, she continued on her way with me itching to follow along after her.

"Thank you for checking on me, Gage," she said from over her shoulder with a sexy smile.

"My *pleasure*, Giselle."

It most certainly was.

Instead of feeling rejected on the walk home, I was hopeful. Maybe she hadn't agreed to see me, but she definitely hadn't told me to stay away from her, either.

And if her shyness in my presence was any indication, I figured I might have a chance with her when I showed up for our date in a few hours from now.

Giselle might not be expecting me to show up

66

so soon, but I was going to use the shit out of my element of surprise.

Giselle

IL ÉTAIT L'HOMME LE PLUS SENSUEL, le plus exaltant et le plus beau que je n'avais jamais vu, embrassé, et couché avec. Mais il ne pouvait pas être à moi. Probablement ne voulant pas être à moi.

Je voulais porter toute sa tristesse sur mes épaules. Je voulais que Gage me regarde chaque jour avec ses aveuglants yeux bleus. Je voulais ce que je ne pouvais pas obtenir.

N'oublie jamais.

Merde.

~pour vous en anglais~

HE WAS THE MOST SENSUAL, exhilarating, and handsome man I'd ever seen, had ever kissed, ever slept with. But he couldn't be mine. Probably didn't want to be mine.

I wanted to take all of his sad onto my shoulders. I wanted to have Gage look at me with those blinding blue eyes daily. I wanted what I could not have.

Never forget.

Shit.

CHAPTER 6

Five hours later.

On the fourth knock, she answered the door wearing a sexy garment that could've been a dress or a slip for all I knew, but she looked fucking hot in it. As I'd hoped, she also wore a very surprised look on her beautiful face.

"What are you doing here, Gage?"

"I'm here for our date, Giselle, and to bring you these." I held out the sketchpads I'd bought from Elysium. "I thought you could put them to good use."

"Thank you, how very kind." Her voice softened as she accepted the sketchpads, but then she pursed her lips, looking past me to see my convertible parked in front of her house. "And if I have plans?"

I leaned against the door frame. "I can wait."

Another one of our cheeky staring contests commenced for about a minute before a smile finally graced her face. "Fine. Give me ten minutes."

And, ten minutes later, she emerged from her house sporting the biggest sunhat I'd ever seen. As she settled in the Jag next to me, I took in her headwear's impressive contours. "At least we'll be covered, rain or shine."

With a giggle, Giselle held up her chin at a tilt. "We will see about that." As I pulled onto the road I could feel her stare. "Do I want to know how you got my address, Gage?"

I turned down the radio—*Every Woman* by The Doors—so I could hear and answer her better. "The art shop," I admitted. "But don't get pissed at the owner. My friend Reid is a real wheeler-dealer."

"Hmm," she said with a brisk nod. "And do I get to find out what exactly our date is for?"

I grinned.

I hadn't even had time to say what we were doing. This whole experience of *her*—her reaction to me showing up at her doorstep, the incredible dress she had on, the fact she'd readily agreed to come with me, had thrown my whole plan into disarray. My original idea had been to make my pitch at her door: a drive to Magnolia Gardens in my convertible for a picnic.

"How long have you been here again?" I asked.

She tucked a section of flickering hair behind her ear. "Not very polite to answer a question with a question, you know, but...for months now."

"So you've probably heard of Magnolia Gardens then?"

She visibly brightened. "Really?"

I winked before reaching over to tug on her hat. "You're wearing just the attire for it too. We won't need to find a tree to sit under."

Giggling, she turned away, happily admiring the landscape.

Once we were outside of the city and the road opened up to basically empty, I opened up the Jag for some real speed. As my foot dug into the gas, the wind picked up. So much so that it threatened to rip off her straw hat completely. Reaching over, I carefully removed it and tucked it under her legs. She smiled at me in thanks.

Feeling the full force of the breeze, she threw her head back and let out a laugh at the sea-blue sky above. "Your car, it's so—"

As the wind whipped her hair behind her, she exhaled on a sigh, "Fantastique."

Once again, the sound of her speaking to me in her native French did something to my insides. "So my car is "fantastique", huh? I'm guessing that means—"

"Silver." Giselle offered helpfully.

For half a second I frowned before seeing her head fall back in that carefree laughter. I shook my head at her. *Every damn time with her.*

"I could not help it." She smiled wide, showcasing a slight space in between her two front teeth, and then sighed dramatically. "Who am I kidding? I'm not sorry, Gage. Your gullibility is too cute."

I kept my eyes on the road, unsure how I was supposed to manage it after that comment sailed off her lovely lips, but luckily we were almost to the gardens. Everything about Giselle had me on full alert and aware of our...connection. Whether either of us could admit there was a *connection* was pointless. Because it was definitely present in every exchange between us, spoken or otherwise. The staring contests, the smiles, the laughs, the teasing, the gentle scolding—all part of what pieced us together. It was so unexpected...and refreshing.

I tried paying for both of us once we made our way inside, but Giselle managed to sneak her own admission when I wasn't looking.

"Is that how they do things in France?" I asked, frowning at her insolent little smirk because she'd messed with my plans.   "The women pay for everything?"

"Maybe."

My hand closed around her waist as I whispered in her ear, "Don't make me pick you up and carry you there myself as punishment."

She gave me a look that was a little bit teasing and a little bit defiant—and really fucking sexy. "And if I scream and shout for police?"

"I don't know about that.   Police here in America aren't the same as in France."

She laughed. "That I do not doubt."

Growing up in Charleston, I'd been to the Gardens at least twenty times over the years, but with Giselle it felt new to me.   She had a knack for pointing out the beauty of our natural surroundings— flower, tree, and sky alike—in a way that made me see it with more color. More…vitality.

By the time we'd reached the willow trees, we were both hot and ready to take a break. The shady spot, along with the picnic basket I'd ordered waiting for us on a blanket, was a welcome sight. It was the first time I'd ever arranged a picnic, and I figured I should do it right if I was going to do it at all. Giselle dropped down onto the blanket with so much enthusiasm her hat fell off. I caught it with my hand and handed it back to her. "I hope there is food in that big basket because I am starved. The flowers were a beautiful distraction, but this looks just as lovely to me right now."

"I agree," I said, only I wasn't referring to our scenic spot *or* the picnic basket. "Why don't you open it and find out."

I could watch her for hours and not get bored. It was the truth. And even though it still shocked the hell out of me, I didn't try to make excuses for the things I felt that I couldn't even name. Honestly, feeling anything at all for a woman I'd known for all of two days was something I never saw coming.

She took my suggestion and opened the lid, revealing wine, cheese, a collection of fruit and other delicious things topped off with a baguette broken in two. "You didn't!" Giselle's delight—her transparent joy—over something as simple as a packed picnic basket only made me want to do more things like this for her. I should be working. I never would have taken days off like this for Cassidy, but for Giselle… She was unreserved with her smiles, happy with simplicity, and seemed to find the good in everything. I couldn't get enough of her.

I reached over and snagged one half of the baguette and took a big bite. "You're right, *I* didn't. *Ted's Butcherblock* packed it up for me. And you should be really happy about that because I am certain Ted does one hell of a better job than I ever could."

"Well, I shall be grateful to Ted then, because he has made us a beautiful picnic, but thank *you*, for arranging it."

We spent the next hour eating and laughing while we chatted under a huge old willow tree with branches weeping so low we were pretty much under our own private umbrella. I started asking questions, hoping she might finally tell me something about her life. "So, you really are an artist—like as a job?"

With two fingers, she wiped the crumbs from her lips and swallowed before responding. "Yes, I really am an artist. Now, do not mistake me, I do not, exactly, 'live large' as you say. But what I do earn is enough to get by."

"How old are you?"

She giggled. "Even I know that asking a lady her age is a *faux pas* in any language, but I don't mind telling you I am recently turned twenty-four."

Young. Younger than I thought.

"Apologies for my breach of manners, but I'm just curious how someone so young can be so free and yet certain of what they want to do." There was something about Giselle that was so diverse and so *physical.* Like a wild creature in its natural habitat. Except her natural habitat was everywhere. She knew where she wanted to be and she just…went there.

"What?" she teased with a gentle prod into my ribs. "Is it so surprising in America to see someone doing what they actually want to?"

"A little bit, yes," I admitted. "But I think it's a dying trend though, just chasing safe jobs. Anyway, I do what I like, mostly."

Nibbling on the edge of a triangle of cheese, she looked up with interest. "What is it you do that you *mostly* like, Gage?"

"I'm a commercial architect, and a partner in a gin distillery with two brothers I've known all my life. I am not as involved in the gin business as my partners, Reeve and Reid Greymont, but my name is on the label."

"Like gin to drink? You make it? What is the name of this special gin, so I can buy it?"

"You don't have to do that. I'll give you a tour of the plant sometime if you're interested. Greymont-Danielson is the name, but our label shows a turquoise 'G' and 'D' on a hexagon bottle."

"Oh my God, that is you, G & D Gin? You are the 'D' with…Danielson? I have seen it in the shops."

I nodded. "Yeah, I'm in involved with the Charleston plant with Reid. There's a larger one in Wilmington that his brother, Reeve runs. But I am an architect by trade…" I trailed off, not sure why beyond the fact I was in the wide-open outdoors, but yet talking about work felt like the walls were closing in on me.

"And why do you *mostly* like what you do?" Giselle missed nothing in conversation I'd noticed. She was an excellent listener and very easy to talk to, so the words sort of tumbled out of my mouth.

"It's being here...in Charleston." I popped a

grape in my mouth and chewed. Swallowed. Giselle waited patiently for me to continue. "I think maybe I need a change...from some things I'd like to forget. I don't know all the answers, but I might want to leave at some point."

Giselle nodded understandingly. "Even if somewhere is our home, and we love it dearly, that does not mean that staying indefinitely is always right." The brown pools of her eyes reflecting the green boughs of the willow tree swaying all around us looked a bit sorrowful.

"Sounds like you know what you're talking about," I said.

"I suppose…" She began tracing the design in the pattern of the blanket with her fingers.

I closed my hand around hers, and when she looked up at me, I asked, "Why did you come here?"

Her lips parted, as if preparing to say something, but then she diverted her attention back to the picnic basket and said, "I do hope Ted has packed us something lovely for dessert."

She doesn't want to tell you. I decided to leave her alone. After all, Giselle and I didn't really know each other, and I still hadn't even told her about…

"I was engaged. Recently."

She turned toward me, the intensity in her eyes understanding and questioning both at the same time. Why did I just say that to her? Was I trying to goad her into a sharing session where I would find out more about her? *I'll tell you mine if you tell me yours*, kind of thing?

Whatever the case, with her intelligent eyes resting on me now, there was no way to sidestep the truth. "It was a...mistake," I said carefully.

She pressed her pink lips together and nodded once, letting it drop.

It was a relief knowing that as far as the sharing game went, Giselle was willing to accept my silence if I was willing to accept hers. For now. *But a part of me wants more.*

"So, what about these for dessert?" I lifted a container of strawberries from the basket and handed it to her.

"I hope there are Twinkies to go with the strawberries," she said.

"Twinkies?"

"Yes, the small cakes in the shape of a tube with cream inside them. They taste good, no?" She looked sincere enough as she described what a Twinkie was, but so many times already...her wicked sense of humor had held the upper hand over me.

"I know what a Twinkie is, Giselle. But what I want to know...are you messing with me right now?" She had to be. A girl like her would not have a Twinkie addiction, would she? I really had no idea with her anymore. Teasing me was one of her best skills.

"No." She shook her head. "I have never tried a Twinkie, but I'd like to. I just thought maybe Ted would have"–she gestured toward the basket and shrugged—"you know, packed them for our dessert." She even looked mildly disappointed as she said, "It is fine if you don't have Twinkies today, but some time I do want to try one."

"If you've never had one, I'm not sure you're going to like them—but they might have Twinkies in the gift shop where they sell snacks. Want to wait here while I go try to find you some?" I guess you could say I'd officially lost my fuckin' mind, with no end in sight to the madness that seemed to overtake me when I was with her. *Twinkies, dude.*

Giselle shook her head and crossed her arms across her chest. "I think you will never learn, Gage Danielson, when I am teasing you, but I will keep testing my theory." She then broke into peals of laughter while trying to get the words out, "Twi—twink—twink-ieees…are j-just the m-most—oorri-blllle—"

I pounced before she could get the rest of words out, pressing her down to the blanket and tickling her until she shrieked, begging me to stop. "I think it's lucky for you I very much like your wicked teasing, Giselle Fleury, but I'll wise up eventually." What I really wanted was to kiss her senseless and then slide her silky dress up her legs, so I could take my sweet time making her shriek for another reason.

But that wasn't exactly possible in public gardens so I made do with the smiling contest we were having instead.

"If you release me, I can make it worth your while."

With the sound of her sexy promise purring in my ears, I eased off her to lie on my side facing her. "I am intrigued."

Giselle put on one helluva sexy show as she pulled a glossy red strawberry out of the bowl and bit down slowly.

Then she brought her berry to my lips and pressed it against them. My eyes locked onto hers; I opened my mouth and bit down. As the sweet taste swept over my tongue, Giselle closed her eyes and sighed, "Strawberries…my favorite."

No sooner had she opened her eyes, she bit into another berry, again offering its smaller form to me. This time, I bit closer, my lips brushing her fingers and holding them there. She didn't move, or take her eyes off me.

And so, the game began. Each shared strawberry brought us closer together. Until there was only one last berry left, which I snatched out of her fingers before she could feed it to me.

I pressed it to her pouting lips this time. Her eyes lowered to the strawberry, then rose back to meet mine, unmoving as she slowly bit into it.

I kissed her just like that—with a strawberry in her mouth.

So, my next taste was of her…of strawberry and want…and Giselle.

We kissed for a long time, savoring the final part of our dessert—the taste of each other.

She was soft in my arms, her skin petal smooth, as if she was a moving, breathing flower that had floated away from inside the gardens. We chased lips and tongues, pressing inside for more and more. Our fingertips stroked and explored, becoming bolder with the swish of wind egging us on. We kissed and rolled on and over each other in the grass. Until we found ourselves somehow in the space behind the huge old tree and a patch of tall sunflowers. A private cove that shielded us from view.

On top of me, Giselle paused to look through the tall flowers which fanned out high above us. "Oh no. Please do not tell me this is the part where the aliens come and get us."

I laughed. *The shit she says…is freaking adorable.*

Leaning over, she delivered another kiss to my lips, her eyes half-lidded in that sultry way that had my cock hard and twitching.

"Seriously, though." Her gaze traced over me in curious strokes. "What happens now?"

There was something of a dare in her question and the way it dropped to my crotch, so I decided to do her one better. Flexing my cock upward against her ass, I said, "Why don't you ask him?"

I saw a bit of fear in the excitement sparking in her brown eyes as she bit down on her lip, but it didn't deter her, because...she reached for the top button of my jeans.

She's not actually...

But my jeans were open, and my briefs were shoved down by her busy, busy hands. Giselle was *going—down—on—me* in a public garden. *Is this real? Is she real?*

"Someone's happy to see me." She took me in her hand and stroked, giving one last sultry look of pure lust before dipping her head down. Her sweet lips met the head of my cock in a wash of feathery sensation that had me groaning incoherently in less than a second.

"...have no idea, baby...fuuuuuuck...ahhh yeah..."

The random words spilling from my mouth as she peppered my cock with kisses only helped to remind me this was really happening. It wasn't just some fantasy I was jerking myself off to. Her tongue took over, hot and wet and stroking up and down my dick.

I had to open my eyes to make sure we were out of sight because my mind was perilously lost in GiselleIsSuckingMyCockLand...and hoping like hell to stay there. But we were securely surrounded by tall

81

sunflowers and a massive tree trunk, hidden from others who might come near. Still dangerously public though as Giselle's expert full lips performed a lewd act upon my eagerly cooperating cock.

I had to grit my teeth and clench my hands into fists to stop myself from losing it on the spot. It wasn't just her open-jawed lips wrapped around my cock, or her tongue-swirling way of sucking me down. No. It was how she moaned around my cock as she did it, as if it was giving her as much pleasure as it was giving me.

And then a hand cupped my balls as sweet series of sucks began. Each one a perfected work of art. Long, painstaking savoring as she sucked all the way down to the base so that the tip of my cock bottomed out against the back of her throat. An actual *moan* came out of her lips as she came up, sending sparks of pleasure firing through my legs.

As her other hand took over the skillful stroking, she was all about quick slickness and flow. Up, down, and around, she sucked. Bobbing her head side to side. Angling her mouth. Seeing her virtually worshipping my cock, it took all I had not to burst on the spot.

And then, when she peeled my cock out of her mouth and started rubbing it over and around her lips, I thought I would die right there.

"So hard…" Her saliva-sweetened smile purred with pleasure.

You're making it so fucking hard.

When she put me in her mouth again, I knew I was close. Clearly, she did too. This time, slow was a thing of the past. Her lips and tongue throttled up and down me fast, deep, and hard.

Blood rushed in my ears.

With the scents of earth and grass and flowers all around me, my eyes opened.

Seeing her on hands and knees working over my cock while sexy moans rolled out of her, I lost it. "Giselle! I'm gonna come."

She didn't back off me, though, even with my desperate warning.

I came. Hard. Spurt after spurt of white-hot ecstasy shot out of me as my fingers sunk into her hair, and she sucked me down hungrily.

Perfect fucking impossible bliss...

And how was this even happening? How was any of this real? This woman? Giselle? This *this*...now?

I sagged back into the soft grass and opened my eyes hazily.

Giselle was wiping the side of her lips daintily with her fingers.

Then she crawled up to meet my lips for a final kiss. As casually as if we'd just finished our meal and left it at that, she draped herself in my arms and looked through the branches at the sunny blue sky. Giselle smiled up at the white clouds and then at me, with nothing but happiness and easiness in the moment. "I love strawberries," she said softly.

I think strawberries love you too.

"When I have you back at my place later I'm returning the favor. Repeatedly."

"Oui, I cannot wait," she said against my neck.

Neither can I, my tempting French beach fairy.

CHAPTER 7

Time passed in a whirlwind after our memorable afternoon at Magnolia Gardens.

Days of working and surfing turned into a week of afternoon trysts and nights with Giselle. The week turned into a month of having her with me on the beach—at my house—in my bed.

Giselle. The addictive enigma who, even after all this time, I still seemed to have only scratched the surface of. My mysterious Gi, as I called her now.

Lying in bed on my side, I could see her through the bedroom's open balcony. The moonlight traced an unearthly glow over her slim curves showing through the transparent nightgown she'd put on.

The sight had me pulling on shorts and leaving the bed to be with her as she leaned on the railing and admired the night sky. When I wrapped my arms around her from behind, she froze for a second as if I'd broken her out of a deep trance. But she then relaxed into my hold, resting her weight against me, our bodies flush.

"I was just thinking." Her voice was clear. As clear as the shining full moon above us. "About how long it has been. About us."

"Me too," I said.

"Must be the full moon," she said with a little laugh.

"One of the first jobs my dad got when he was in his early twenties was at a corrections facility. He said it was at a full moon when the great majority of the fights and madness occurred like clockwork."

She turned her head to meet my eyes.

"The question is, what kind of madness does it mean for us now?"

The challenge I saw in her eyes suddenly weighed me down. Although I didn't want to let go of her, I slumped back to sit on the end of the chaise lounge.

"You know, it feels like there's enough madness already." She waited for me to say more. "These

86

feelings—I mean...they're just...not at all what I expected."

She continued with her moon-gazing. "Not what you expected in a good way? Or bad?"

Pushing upright, I caught her by the waist and flopped back into the chaise, bringing her down with me.

"Bad, obviously." I nuzzled and kissed her neck. "So terribly bad."

She laughed lightly. "Me too. What a summer being stuck with this Gage guy."

As we laughed, she eased herself back, until her head rested on my shoulder. "Seriously, though. When I came to Charleston, I never expected...to find...someone like you."

Her hand rested on top of mine, facing forward as we held them up, and I could see how much smaller her delicate fingers were compared to mine. Fingers that drew portraits, that touched my body with perfect skill, that I loved to have in my mouth and kiss.

"Same. When I met you, I was in a low place mentally. My ex and I had just recently broken up and..."

"You don't have to tell me if you don't want to."

The free pass was implicit in her words even though I wouldn't accept it. Not this time.

I focused on the glossy circle of the moon and stroked her silky hair through my fingers.

"We fought for more than half of our relationship. About the stupidest things, too, like...my socks on the floor. Although I think, deep down, all that was because of the real problems, the ones we barely talked about. I couldn't open up to her."

Giselle stiffened against me slightly, but she didn't speak. She was in listening mode. And since this was something I wanted her to know about me, I kept on talking. Because this wasn't really about her—it was about *me*. I was saying these things out loud for myself.

"In the end, she left me. And she was right to."

"But didn't you say that she was—"

I clasped her hand in mine. "Okay, so she did it in the shittiest way possible, by giving me a page of handwritten hate-speech and running off with one of my friends, who she'd already been fucking." I let out a half-laugh that had been trapped deep in my chest, but now seemed to want to be free. "But the past months have given me perspective. That it was for the best. That Cassidy and I, we weren't right for each other. She knew it, and, deep down, I knew it too." I shrugged. "I guess I just figured our relationship was normal. What you did. Found a person you were more or less compatible with and settled down. Built a life that was better together than if you were alone. Whenever I saw those romantic comedy movies, I'd always roll my eyes. I never thought it was possible to feel—"

"That strongly about someone." Instead of sounding cheerful, Giselle's whisper was desolate…like a death sentence. And yet, she snuggled against me, and held me tight. "I'm so happy I met you, Gage."

Her words pricked my heart.

Suddenly, despite being outside in the open air, I felt stifled. I cared deeply about Giselle. And so, the right thing would be to tell her about the type of man I was. Clearly the *right thing* to do, but it felt agonizing doing it.

"Giselle." I took both her hands in both of mine and pressed them tight. "I need to say something."

My nerves left me as soon as I made the decision. How could I even know Giselle was thinking that far ahead? We'd only been together for one month, after all. Maybe she wouldn't mind what I was going to say. She'd never mentioned exes or marriage or children.

After a few seconds of deliberating over the right words, it occurred to me there weren't any.

"One thing my ex said in her letter was definitely right. I don't think marriage is in the cards for me."

An overpowering silence screamed between us.

Giselle didn't react as I expected she might. No piercing wit or sarcastic teasing. No dismissive little laugh. Only a cool solemnity that came over her features. Her eyes closed for a moment, and then when she opened them again, they were resolute as she spoke into the cool night air.

"I have something to tell you too."

CHAPTER 8

"**M**y visa is expiring. I have to go back."

Her words were logical, and yet, they wouldn't compute in the structured confines of my brain no matter how many times I ran through them.

"I have to return to France in two days. I am sorry."

Two days? What the fuck?!

She twisted around, finally with the dejection in her eyes I'd expected. "I could not manage to figure out how to break it to you. I kept meaning to, and then…"

Catlike, she left my lap and made her way to the balcony railing. I went to the opposite side and leaned over as far as I could without falling, half suspended in open air.

A Molotov cocktail of emotions boiled through me, pushing me under in a sea of shock. Fury, despair, fear. But what did I expect? That Giselle would stick around indefinitely when she didn't even fucking live here?

As I accepted her news, I realized I was lucky it had ended like this, instead of the *Cassidy-way,* with another woman disillusioned.

I had to face facts: there wasn't an exhaustive supply of women who would be content to just pass time with me, knowing any "relationship" we had wouldn't really go anywhere. I knew all too well how young girls were raised, even today in the so-called era of the "modern woman"...on Hallmark Channel movies and Instagram wedding envy. I'd seen it with my friends, Paul and Isa, and I'd seen it with Cassidy. I had no doubt that most women, apart from a very few, would have the same expectations in mind.

Not that that had been the problem here, clearly. *I have to return to France in two days.* Christ, did she really have to break this to me so last minute? Sure, this whole time it had felt like things with Giselle had been too good to last, but still. I'd thought I would've at least had enough time to reconcile myself to her leaving when the time came. Say a proper goodbye.

"Do you want me to go?"

That she had to ask me at all cut me off at the knees, because there was something deeply wrong with me. I *should* be able to tell her how I felt about her. I *should* be able to say, "No, I don't want you to go back to France and leave me," but I didn't say any of that. *Two days. In two days, she'll be gone...*

I closed the distance between us and pulled her into my arms. "On your second to last night here? Not a chance."

Before my eyes, her face transformed. The statuesque coolness melted away into a soft smile. "So, what does that mean, Gage?"

"What that means"—I leaned in to give her a quick kiss on the lips—"is that we still have one more day together."

She arched a brow. "What will we do?"

I shook my head. "All you need to know is this"—I tightened my hold around her— "tomorrow belongs to me."

There was something almost tragic in the smile she gave me. Nonetheless, she pressed her sweet lips to mine and kissed me until I took her back to bed.

I stroked, kissed, sucked, licked, fucked—*every* thing she loved to pull the two words from her that *I craved* above all others.

"Oh, *oui*..."

"RISE AND SHINE, GI."

Giselle's eyes fluttered open, then closed just as briefly. Settling myself in the bed beside her, I carefully balanced the plate on my bare chest and speared a sausage with my fork.

"I guess I'll just finish this fine breakfast myself if you're not hungry."

Like a switch being flipped, Giselle's eyes snapped open and she let out a huff of annoyance. When I kissed her cheek, a pouty frown crept over her face.

In the early days, Giselle had warned me she was not a morning person. "Gi in the morning," we called it. I took the opportunity to tease her out of it most days, but this morning I found her black temper incredibly cute.

Wriggling herself upright, Giselle accepted the fork I offered her and took a tentative bite, looking like the French sex goddess she was...with the sheet about to slip below her left breast as she ate her breakfast in bed. *I'm going to miss this so much.*

"One question," she said, in between bites.

"Just one?" I teased.

Giselle's obsession with questions was no secret. She enjoyed nothing more than to hit me with five or so questions at a time, fascinated by the responses.

She jabbed out her fork slightly, as if considering. "Just one—for now."

"Ask away, then." I tugged on the sheet and made it fall.

"Do I get to know what we are doing today?"

Leaning in, I kissed the tip of her nose, and then moved down to give some attention to her perfect and gorgeous breasts, smiling all the while. "This is how it starts."

IT FELT LIKE DÉJÀ VU ALL OVER AGAIN flying down the highway in my Jag, Giselle wearing her spaceship of a sun hat looking beautiful and happy.

Although I wasn't taking her to Magnolia Gardens again. Today we were going somewhere she'd told me she very much wanted to visit but had never been able to go. The zoo.

Her excitement when I pulled into the parking area was the reaction I hoped for, but I know we were both feeling the urgency of time winding down for us. There was only a little bit left, and I wanted to make sure she was doing something enjoyable with the few hours that remained.

Still, seeing her as overjoyed at the sight of a doe lying with her fawn, I couldn't regret even a moment of being in a public place with her when I only wanted her all to myself. I had hoped that there was a chance we could figure something out after she returned to France. She *could* come back to the US again after she fulfilled the requirements of her visa in France. *She could…if she wanted to.*

"Just *look* at the bébé." God, I was going to miss how she found joy in simple things. It was how Giselle existed in life—laughing and dancing her way through it.

Leaning in, I whispered, "Hate to say it, but I think a baby deer is your true spirit animal, rather than the sparrow."

"Maybe yes," she said. She rested her eyes on me and became thoughtful. "And what would your spirit animal be I wonder.? Something proud and solemn I'd say. Like a stag watching over his deer family."

More of our past flashed in my head—the last time she had looked at me so deeply, at the beach, when she had first drawn me and made her less-than-flattering assessment. *Hard. Proud. Closed off.*

"Sorry if I was a bit blunt that first time I drew you," she said softly.

"How did you know I was thinking about that? Can you read minds too?"

She laughed and shook her head. "No, I am not a mind reader, but I can connect the dots much of the time."

I'd have to agree with her. Even now, as she looked at me, her eyes appeared to have an all-seeing gift. "Do you still see me that way?" I asked with a casualness I didn't feel.

She frowned and bit her lip. Not a good sign—

"In some ways, yes." She slipped her hand around mine and squeezed it. "In a lot of ways, though, no." Her shy gaze found mine. "When we spend a lot of time together, sometimes I feel like you are a different person. So warm and genuine and..." Her face scrunched up, and she slapped a palm to her lips. "There I go again, insinuating that normal you is this cold monster."

I gave her a smile that I knew was only for her. Nobody else had a chance in hell of making me smile after pointing out my faults to my face. "Don't worry about it."

She pulled her hand from mine. "No, I *will* worry about it. I need to make you understand. How...I cannot pinpoint what it is, but sometimes when you have been with me for a long time or"— she peered up at me and held my face in both of her hands—"Like now. Your eyes look different. Happier." *Because you make me fucking happy, and I hate that you're leaving.*

"Because I am happy when I'm with you, but please don't let it go to your head, Frenchy."

She pushed up on her toes and kissed me. "I will not, Surfeur américain."

The rest of our time sped by far too fast. More cute animals to admire. More kisses shared along with some strawberries when we ate lunch. Finally, when she slumped her head on my shoulder wearily, I swept her off her feet and carried her to the car as she squealed in protest.

Inside the car, I begged for forgiveness in the form of kisses.

"Stop, Gage." Her face the textbook definition of absolute glee, told a completely different story. "I mean it."

"Your mouth says stop, but your body says go," I said, flipping up her poufy skirt. She only laughed more uproariously. As I traced my hands up her thighs, I admitted, "I guess you're right. We need to get started on our grand finale before the day is over."

Even though I was laughing as I said it, as was she...the words sliced into my heart with painful precision.

HOURS LATER, AFTER WINING AND DINING HER, and our time was ticking away too fucking fast, I finally had her where I really wanted her. The two of us alone in my house with the cool night air blowing in through the open balcony doors.

"Oh, what is this?" Giselle asked when she spotted the teal-and-gold-wrapped gift on my bed.

My hand on the small of her back urged her forward. "It's just something for you to put to good use, and I know you will." No way was I ever going to admit that I'd actually told Old Bat Art Lady to find gift wrap that matched the color of Giselle's crochet dress and the dark gold of her hair the first time I saw her waving at me on the beach. That secret would have to go with me to my grave.

The image of the very first time you saw her will too.

Giselle began opening it carefully, as if to preserve the pretty paper, then abruptly said, "Oh, what the hell," before the rest of it was ripped away in a haphazard second.

When she saw what it was, she fell silent. Almost in slow motion, she turned to me and did something I'd never seen her do before.

Her eyes filled with tears and she...cried.

Slowly she sat on my bed, holding my gift in her lap like it was the most precious treasure. "Oh, Gage, you didn't..."

I sat down beside her as she focused her teary eyes on the drawing set I'd found at Elysium—a tiered mahogany box containing a selection of the highest quality graphite, charcoals and sepias money could buy.

"But I did."

Giselle traced her fingers over the glossy wooden box lovingly before hugging it to her chest. "Thank you, thank you, thank you!" She leaned into me and gave me the sweetest thank-you kiss I'd ever received from giving a gift. As we drew apart, her shining eyes still locked on me, she said, "No one has ever been better to me than you have."

Her brutally simplistic words left me speechless, because I didn't feel like I'd done much for her at all. A few dinners and some outings, where if I hadn't watched her carefully, she'd have snuck to pay while I was distracted by something? That was what she meant? She was so far off from my truth if that was what she believed. Giselle was the one who'd given me far more than I could ever give to her. And that was the part that bothered me the most...because I didn't know what to say or how to explain it in words. *No one has ever been better...* And there was so much finality in her words. She was leaving.

But being the mind reader she was, Giselle caught on. She sensed my discomfort and took me out of that uncomfortable place in my head and replaced it with something much better.

Carefully placing the drawing set on the bedside table, she then climbed to the middle of the bed and spread herself out like a decadent feast ready to be devoured.

"How may I *ever* thank you?"

The sultry roll of her *r* 's had me instantly hard. "I can think of some ways."

"I think you can too," she said with eyes half hooded and an arch of her back that let me know her pussy was already wet.

I crawled up on the bed beside her and slid my

hands up her short skirt for the second time today, hyper aware that I wouldn't be able to do it again after this. I paused to admire the sight of her in nothing more than the lacy pink panties she had on, but not for long. I was on a mission critical with not a minute to waste. "As much as I love this view, I think—no—*I know* that these have got to go, baby."

She responded by arching her back and shoving her tits out...but best of all, by moaning for me in French. My favorite. I slipped my fingers underneath the lace and pulled them down her long lovely legs to unveil my stunning prize.

Then I slid my hands to the inside of her knees and spread her wide open. Yep, her pussy was wet...and very much in need of my mouth. As I descended to kiss and lick her to a perfectly pitched crying orgasm, in French of course, one thought looped through my head on repeat: *How will I survive never doing this with her again?*

The knowledge that this was the last time was felt by both of us. So, while the sex took on a sort of harried urgency, we also relished each and every moment. After I made her come the first time, I stripped away every remaining stitch of clothing from her body until she was naked and perfect just as God had made her. I did the same with my own clothes while she watched until we were a matched set. We set out to savor the touch of our lips and tongues across every inch of skin we could kiss. My lips found a mole on the back of Giselle's left upper thigh I'd never noticed before. It felt cruel that I only discovered it now.

My lips skated down the line of her spine and settled on the dip above her ass, and then lower. The desperate moans escaping her pretty lips were music to my ears.

But it was her *Oh, oui!* that I lived for. That was when I knew I was really getting somewhere.

So, when I pulled her to her knees and opened her up to lick at her clit from behind, it was those two words I was gunning for. Even as my fingers slipped into her slick pussy, I didn't let up on my stroking until I heard her say them. The sound was as sweet as heaven's doors opening just for me.

Her golden hair had tumbled free of her ponytail, and now wildly shook as she contorted herself in abandon. Giselle was all about expression…in everything she did in her life. Sexual pleasure was no different an expression for her than the joy in blowing me in a patch of sunflowers. It was beautiful to witness, and I felt like she'd given me a precious gift to be able to be the one to help her with that expression.

When I finally pressed my cock into her sweet, sweet self, that thought disintegrated. All thought did. Thought was transmuted to sensation, two bodies learning and flowing as one. *This is the last time.* This feasting and clashing of kisses. This stroking and claiming and owning of bodies. This feeling of hands and fingers engaged in a dance nearing its inevitable end.

And, amidst it all, the omnipresent clash of us coming together, the in, the out. More and more, farther and deeper, her tight heat, my penetrating cock. Together. How we were meant to be for this perfect, last time.

And yet, it was too divinely designed to stop. We both moved with a sort of learned carefulness. To make it good, but not too good. Perfect, but not perfect past the point of control. Because then, it would be over. *This is the last time.*

So, we flowed from position to position like synchronized dancers who'd gone through this a hundred times, until we could make it look seamless. Fucking her became…life. Because every part of Giselle responded exquisitely to my touch. And yet, when she started clasping and grooving my dick into her, and new heights of pleasure started to grip me, I knew with a pang of regret, there was no putting off where this was headed anymore.

Not anymore. Not this finale of finales. This inevitable ending that was in our beginning. This building and growing and becoming.

Oh, oui became my refrain as we kept on joining into each other, merging into one unending moan. Flowing us onward. Surging me forward. My dick acting of its own accord. In and out and deeper. More and more. Neurons firing and nerve endings blasting. And through it all, *us*, coming as one. One organism. One urge. One being satisfying itself and then, finally…one release.

Her cry seemed to come from outside of her and my own groan was something I'd never heard before. I lost control completely, and my body flailed with hers, against hers, *as* hers.

Finally, it was over. And fuck if that didn't feel so incredibly wrong. Over. Finished. Last. *I hate it.*

I held her in my arms. I didn't dare speak, lest I voiced the trite thing vibrating through my whole body, the only thing that would've been right to say: *I never want to let you go.*

I WOKE WARM. She was still in my arms. My Frenchy beach fairy was snuggling against me in my bed. Everything felt wholly right and quietly, peacefully, still.

Except…I needed to piss, so I reluctantly disentangled myself from her sleeping form. When I left the bathroom, my bare feet made contact with something. In the sliver of moonlight sneaking through my curtains, I could just make out…my dirty socks.

Smiling grimly, I took one step more, then paused. Cursing to myself, I bent down, grabbed them, strode over to the hamper, and chucked them in.

There.

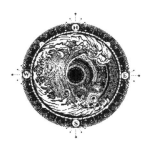

CHAPTER 9

I woke up cold.

As soon as my eyes opened, I knew. She'd left. Giselle had gone without even saying goodbye.

Although I did have her cell number by now, I didn't bother, because I knew she'd already shut it off. No, I was almost certain where I would find her.

Tossing on whatever clothes in my bedroom floor radius seemed to take half an instant and several decades too long. Racing out to my car took too fucking long too.

Only a few minutes later, once I merged onto the busy highway, did I realize what I'd been in a race with: my sense of certainty. And if the paperweight lodged in my chest as I stared unseeing at the stream of cars ahead of me was any indication, I had lost.

After breaking the news that she was leaving, Giselle had made no real mention of her flight. What sort of moron hadn't asked her for that vital fucking information? Or would have figured the best plan was to head to the airport—not her place—first? *I'm so fucked.*

I glanced at my watch for the fifth time. Yep, it was 12:17 p.m. already—I'd somehow managed to sleep in until noon. *Fuck.* At least if Giselle wasn't at the airport, then I could probably catch her at her place still, right? Unless she was on her way out at this very moment and I managed to miss her by seconds. *Epically fucked.*

Whatever the case, all I knew was that I had to try to see her again and chastising myself as I sped along a busy highway wouldn't do me any favors.

Inside a few minutes and one shitty parking job later, I thanked the gods that Charleston didn't have numerous terminals like a bigger airport. Here I was, the only terminal Giselle could be in if she was at this airport and hadn't gone through TSA yet. She'd be flying to New York most likely because there were no direct flights to Europe from Charleston. My eyes slid from one faceless person to another, rapid-fire, seeing only that they weren't her.

There was a Caviar Banana stand (whatever the hell that was), a wooden-paneled stand called Harvest Grounds, and then there, in the corner, looking almost as stupefied to see me as I was her...*my French beauty.* She looked delighted, and upset, and contrite all at once as I rushed over to her.

When all those emotions had washed away, all that was left was a miserable expression.

"I am sorry, Gage." She looked at me with her eyes up and her head lowered, like a child about to be scolded. "I am very terrible at goodbyes."

Frozen motionless, half-believing my incredible luck of finding her here, I threw my arms around her and pressed her to me tight. "I'm just glad I caught you," I said against her neck, inhaling the scent of her so I could remember.

She buried her head in my chest as our bodies eased into each other. I felt woozy, sick, like if I peeled away from this woman, my body parts would fall to the floor.

The motherfucking loudspeaker boomed above us, "1:20 p.m. flight to Paris through JFK now boarding. Please proceed to gate—"

Giselle eased out of my embrace and hiked her bag over her shoulder. "That is me. Late as always."

And yet, she didn't move. We stared at each other, as if willing the other to make the move, say the words. The right ones that didn't exist that would make this better. *But what? What was the point? Her flight's been called. This is it.*

Giselle tried to smile, but her lips only drooped more before she shook her head and said, "Au revoir, mon beau surfeur." She pressed a finger to her lips and then blew a kiss to me before turning and walking toward the security checkpoint. My understanding of French had improved enough that I knew what she'd just said to me. She'd said it before. *Goodbye, my beautiful surfing man.*

I watched her go in a dreamlike state, realization descending on me gradually. The one thing that mattered. What I should've said.

Gi…I love you.

But I'd let it go too long…and now it was too late.

Those were fairy-tale heartfelt words for a different time, different place, and most of all…different person. *Not me.* Not the hard, proud, ever-closed-off disappointment of Gage Danielson.

Giselle had even said it herself. *Sad.* Because without her, that was what I was. Would be. *Fuck.*

GISELLE

M'ÉLOIGNER DE LUI ÉTAIT probablement la chose la plus pénible que je n'avais jamais faite. Mais j'ai vu son visage, et il ne pouvait pas exprimer ce qu'il ressentait pour moi.

Si Gage m'aime vraiment, il peut me le dire. J'en mérite autant.

Même lorsqu'il y a tant à donner à l'intérieur de lui, il a toujours peur.

Mon beau surfeur ne connaît pas encore la profondeur de ce qu'il pourrait offrir, si seulement il permettait à l'amour de traverser la douleur qui habite son cœur.

N'oublie jamais.

Je ne t'oublierai jamais, Gage. Mon amour.

~pour vous en anglais~

WALKING AWAY FROM HIM was probably the hardest thing I've ever had to do. But I saw his face, and he could not say whatever he does feel for me.

If Gage does love me, he can say it to me. I deserve that.

Even when there is so much inside of him to give, he is still afraid.

My beautiful surfing man just does not yet know the depths of what he could give if only he would allow the love to break through the hurt that lived in his heart.

Never forget.

I will never forget you, Gage, my love.

CHAPTER 10

Four days later.

"**Y**ou holding up okay?"

I frowned as I lolled back onto my bed, closing my eyes. Although Gray's call was our first talk since our meal at Jazz Street a little over a month ago, I could guess that Reid had filled him in on all the Giselle details he'd pried out of me since her departure.

Couldn't have even one week to myself to process things before my friends came crowding in. Nope. Reid had shown up unannounced the very next day after Giselle left, and seeing my dejected state, had point-blank guessed the whole thing.

Clearing my dry throat, I lied, "I'm okay, Gray."

"Good. At least it was only a month."

"Yeah," I echoed hollowly.

A month, I reminded myself. *Only a month.* Not long enough to truly know anyone…or to fall in love with them. Whatever I'd felt for Giselle was just lust in its purest form. *You keep telling yourself that, asshole.*

It was common knowledge that those spur-of-the- moment, love-at-first-sight Vegas weddings never worked out. Not for rich and famous celebrities, and definitely not for us regular people. No matter how strongly I believed I cared for Giselle, all it could be was simple head-over-heels lust. *Liar. Just keep on lying to yourself, motherfucker.*

"How are things with you?" I asked. My attempt at being a decent friend, before I indulged in bad manners crying about my life without asking about his.

"Really great, actually." His sorry tone set my teeth on edge. "Reese is getting impatient for the baby to be born. She's cranky and uncomfortable and in need of constant reassurance that she'll be a good mom, and that I'll still love her if she weighs a few pounds more than she did before. Shit like that. And it's just…great…"

I tuned Gray out as I pretend-listened to him tell me how "great" it was to be with the one you love and living through the milestones of life I'd probably never experience. I started rifling through the contents of my bedside drawer as a distraction. It was a catchall for pencils, receipts and random notes, so when my hand made contact with something unfamiliar, I pulled it out.

A piece of drawing paper from Elysium.

"Gage?" Gray asked.

I turned the paper over and saw words written in a familiar hand.

"Yeah?" I answered on autopilot.

"Reid's dating this new girl. She's Brazilian and so tall she has to—"

I stopped listening to whatever the fuck he was saying because…I was reading the poem in my hand.

love

is not just a word with you

love

is your sweet kiss at the small of my back

love

is a new smile in your eyes on our third hour mark

love

is our dirty socks entwined in the hamper

love

is just you

I read it again and again. The answer to a question I hadn't even asked her started strumming through my veins.

"Sorry, Gray," I told him, "Just realized something. Talk to you later, brother."

I lifted the paper to my lips, pressed and held it there. My eyes closed, and I breathed deeply in and out.

It was obvious now. What my body had known, but my mind had taken too fucking long to figure out.

I *loved* Giselle, and she *loved* me too. *Thank God she had the courage to say it.*

I didn't know what in hell that would mean for me now, except that by letting her go, I'd made the biggest mistake of my life.

So now, the only thing for me to do was to set it right.

Later that evening.

THE FLIGHT TO PARIS was one level beyond unbearable.

Unable to secure anything in business class, my last-minute seat assignment had me wedged between a tired mother, her cranky toddler, and a very large man on the aisle in a flop sweat. With the toddler shrieking and the man's prolific sweaty rolls angling for me, it seemed like they were in an unofficial competition as to who could make the flight more awful.

I slapped headphones on and cranked up the music...and thought about how Giselle would make this hideous experience somehow laughable— something funny to reflect upon at a later time. My French beach fairy possessed special skills like that.

When my seat mate fell asleep and began snoring (and sweating) on my shoulder, no matter how many times I prodded him off, he won.

Seven-hours-and-twenty-minutes of claustro-phobic hell later, it all came to a welcome end when I stepped out into the early morning Paris sunshine. I hadn't been to Paris in years, but I soon began to align myself with the layout of the city. My chest still had the ache firmly in place, but maybe it was eased somewhat in knowing I was on the same continent as Giselle again.

The taxi line out of the airport wasn't exactly a quick affair, and the trip into the city took a while, but I knew where I was headed. Although calling it a "lead" was being generous.

"I just cannot get enough of drawing at the Tuileries Garden," she said. "My favorite spot is under those perfect rows of trees, in the shade." A wistful smile came over her face as she remembered. "Before I left, it had gotten to the point where I had named all of the trees and learned the names of some of the regulars. There was Maurice, the little old man who talked to himself and even to me too if I bothered him

enough. There was Hillary, the middle-aged woman with the long winding yellow scarf, who came at twelve o'clock for one hour precisely each and every day. There was Winston the squirrel, who would stop by every so often to nibble at my sunflower seeds."

So, to the Tuileries I went.

Unlike my expectations, most people I asked for directions knew English and were very polite to use it with me. Although I'd been to Paris before, I'd never gone to the Tuileries. So, I followed their instructions and sure enough, when my squint stopped on green that extended as far as I could see, I knew I was golden. A quick walk through the gardens found them far bigger than I expected.

But I was fatigued to nearly collapsing-level proportions, so I stopped in at a nearby express grocery store to deal with the basics. After loading up with several incomprehensible but still clearly ham packages, Doritos, some oranges, and a container of strawberries, I hit up the bathroom.

There, after washing the strawberries in the sink, I popped one in my mouth.

"I just love strawberries." she'd said amidst the sunflowers. It had only been a month ago, but it seemed like a different era entirely.

Quit fucking crying about it and get your sorry ass moving, fool.

Determined not to waste another second, I strode outside and into the park. There, I began my search, which also doubled as sight-seeing. Now I could see it through her eyes just as she'd sketched it for me in my mind.

I meandered past several giddily spurting fountains, brigades of expertly crafted statues, a ton of painstakingly tended gardens with flowers every shade of the rainbow, and an infinite number of trees.

After an exhaustive search, peering around every shrub and oak, examining every vaguely Giselle-resembling girl who passed me by, there was nothing left to do but camp out by the long rows of trees Giselle had told me about. The shade was where I slouched for my wait.

Here I would sit, and here I would stay. This was the best—the only—chance I really had for running into Giselle. *This will work. She'll come.*

A few hours later, down to my last chewy ham slice with the sun nosing down the horizon, I wasn't so sure. I'd been sitting on this uncomfortable patch of grass for what had to be four hours now. Despite the vigilant and borderline insane way I'd been staring holes and occasionally following any woman that even passably resembled Giselle, I hadn't seen her. So far, the police hadn't showed up to ask me to leave, so I counted my blessings, even though it wasn't much.

Although I'd had ample time to imagine what Giselle might be doing while I sat waiting in the Tuileries hoping to find her. No matter what odd charming situations I half-pictured in my mind's eye, they always came back to the same image of her eating strawberry pancakes in her flat while looking out over Paris. Yep, that was the only other "lead" I had on her. Giselle lived in the city and apparently loved it.

So, all I had to do was search out every twenty-four-year-old artist living in downtown Paris... *What an easy fucking task that'll be.* I prayed it wouldn't come to that. The Tuileries was my best chance.

Scowling, I swatted away a fly descending on what was left of my half-eaten strawberries. The ants, flies, and the occasional bumblebee had long since discovered my presence and had banded together to drive me insane.

"M. vous doivez partir." A man decked out like a swanky mall cop leaned over to give me the brunt of his judgy well-mustached frown.

In response to my blank face, he let out an impatient sigh.

"The park is closed," he said in a heavily accented voice, stabbing his finger out to drive the point home. "You must leave."

THE NEXT MORNING, I WAS UP EARLY, wolfing down my croissant as I barreled down the stairs two at a time. Surprisingly rested after sleeping so well in my room at Hôtel Juliana, I decided it was because I was now in the same city where *she* was.

Outside, speed walking was essential, since the sidewalks were already flocked with people.

About twenty minutes later, I was back at *my* spot. Parked in the very same indentation in the grass where my ass had been situated less than twelve hours prior. Flanked by my sentinel of perfect tree lines and a grasping, increasingly diminishing *hope*.

And so the hours slowly crept along as I leaned on the tree and a parade of *not-hers* passed by. Most looked to be tourists. Fascinated timeworn men, bored adolescent girls.

Seeing a lilac-haired one stride past without so much as lifting her eyes off the screen made pain scrape through me. Giselle and I had talked about that, one night—people barely living because they were so concentrated on their phones—after I'd nonchalantly mentioned never seeing her on her own Motorola.

"The whole phone thing, it is like a screen for the present moment," she said. *"To face the world head-on, to give it one instant or iota of their full attention, is something most people today cannot bear. So, they glaze it away. Glue their gaze and minds to the screen. Scrolling, scrolling to infinity. Maybe a picture, a few texts saying nothing in response to less. When you think about it, it is nothing more than a smart, sad strategy. Always being halfway in this world and halfway in that, so there is no room."*

"Room for what?" I asked.

A shadow passed over her face. "For the thoughts they

cannot bear creeping in."

As I stared glumly ahead, the thoughts I hadn't wanted to face hit me square in the gut. Cassidy had been right about me. That in the end, even when I'd met a girl I really did care for, or *love*, I'd messed it up.

Maybe I was doomed to be alone.

And Giselle? I'd never found out what had driven her to Charleston so impulsively. Why hadn't I pushed until she'd told me? We'd spoken about many things, but had we ever truly gone beneath the surface? Had she wanted me to?

Something in me ached with recognition. Regret over what could've saved everything. Maybe if we'd bonded over her intimate secret, maybe she would've stayed. Maybe I would've realized sooner what she meant to me.

The sun seesawing from one horizon to the other was my indication of time passing and marching forward. When its shining orb began its inevitable descent, so too did my last dregs of hope. This was it, then.

She isn't coming.

I'd been wrong. Maybe Giselle was staying with some friends on the opposite side of town. Maybe she wasn't even here in Paris. She'd once told me that her father lived on a farm in the countryside and had started a second family with his new young wife after her mother died. Maybe she'd gone to visit them. After all that had happened with her, all I could really admit to myself with complete certainty was that I didn't really know her as well as I should've.

When my eyes stopped on the seventh Giselle look-alike of the day, I tossed my last slice of orange in my mouth. The moment seemed ironically symbolic, watching the wind ruffle the golden waves of her long hair as she paced down the aisle of trees, toward me. My last bite of orange, the last sight of a Giselle look-alike. It was time to go; I could see that now. I'd have to try to find her another way.

I rose, and the Giselle look-alike stopped.

"It is you," she breathed.

I gaped at her. At her green dress fluttering in the breeze. Her parted lips that couldn't seem to settle on the smile her eyes were shining with. Those eyes, that weren't brown as I remembered them. Now, surrounded by so much green, they were too. Dark green shining emeralds.

"Gi." I rasped out her name. I did not believe it was her at first. Couldn't fucking believe it. I'd seen too many girls with the same hair dancing in the wind. I'd seen too many girls with bohemian style and an unhurried step. Too many girls *who were not her.*

"What are you doing here?"

Giving you my heart.

Still, her face couldn't decide whether to be

surprised, happy, or both.   She looked a little shocked.

Taking both her hands into mine, I said, "I'm here for you."

CHAPTER 11

"What are you saying?" she asked quietly.

Under the view of those candid, expectant eyes, there was only room for one thing. The truth.

"I'm saying that I'm not fine with leaving things as they were." I held her gaze. "Or ending things—ending us. I don't know how, but I do know *who*. For me, it's you, Gi. As soon as you left and I found your poem, I understood that I don't want to live without you for even one more day—"

She stopped my words in their tracks with two fingers to my lips.

The wind had stopped blowing. All was still as though we needed the calm to speak.

"There is still so much you do not know about me, Gage." She was guarded, but truthful. I could live with truth, though. The truth would get us to where we needed to go together.

I raised her hand that was still clasped in mine to my lips and kissed it, breathing in the sweet scent of her skin, knowing relief for the first time in days. "But I've got time." I winked and gave her a grin hoping she remembered.

She bit on her bottom lip as a pretty smile bloomed on her face. "I think you've used that same line with me before."

"It's a good one…and if it works…well, then I'm using it on you, Frenchy."

She laughed softly. "Would *mon beau surfeur* like to come to my flat?"

"Oui." *He would very much like to come to your flat. He would very much like for you to* come *in your flat, too.*

HER PARISIAN FLAT was close to how I'd imagined it. From the old limestone walls to the eclectic interior. A bed with tie-dye sheets of teal-blues, lime-greens and canary-yellow, and presiding in the center of the room, her easel.

I'd never been in her room in Charleston, now

that I thought of it. It'd never really crossed my mind because when I wasn't working—and God, had I become an excellent delegator—we'd spent nearly all our time together at the beach house or on the actual beach. Her sketching while I surfed. But being here, in the place where she *lived*, seemed far more intimate than I could've asked for.

She flopped down on her bed and gestured for me to sit.

I sat beside her.

The silence in the room was keen. Giselle clasped and unclasped her hands, wrestling with something painful within herself.

Every atom in me burned to say something, to console her. To tell her whatever she had to say was safe with me. *I* was safe. That the strength of the adoration I felt for her wasn't the sort some dark new information would extinguish. Even if I wanted it to feel different about her, I couldn't. I understood that now.

One glance of her wretched face indicated that right now my part was to stay silent. This was Giselle's choice, and her fight to fight, her story to tell.

Finally, she spoke.

"I went to Charleston to get away."

She drew her fingers through her hair, and when they caught a snag she ripped them free, shaking her head in frustration. She let out a tortured sigh, as if finally accepting the imperfect narrative she needed to tell.

"Henri and I met when I was sixteen, at a time when my mother was dying of cancer, and I was angry at having to lose her. A few months was all it took for us to form a bubble between ourselves and the rest of the world and ourselves. I moved out, I dropped out of school. We had the most insane lives, like in a storybook."

A bitter smile I wanted to kiss away until she was back to her usual carefree happiness marred her beautiful face, but she had so much more to say. And…more importantly, for her, I had time to listen.

"Dancing and partying and drinking all night. It was all such brilliant fun that I almost didn't notice what was happening. How my friends were dropping away. My life. My art." She shook her head. "He started stealing to support us, and he got pretty good at it, I guess. The years blurred together, and our bubble shrank and shrank and shrank. Until there was nothing left for me but him. Until our lives were so stifled and limited that we had no choice but to hate each other. He became irritable and tyrannical, blowing up at any wrong thing I said." She closed her eyes, her lower lip trembling as if she were experiencing it in this very moment. "The first few years, I tried to leave. That was the saddest part of all. Wherever I went, whoever I stayed with…he would somehow find out. He would know. Every time he showed up with his grim apologetic smile, familiar kind eyes, and I figured it was a sign. That someone who fought so hard for me could not possibly be wrong."

She shuddered, her head wilting in defeat.

"And yet, how wrong I was. The longer I spent with him, the more I whittled away into nothing. I became bone thin, quiet, depressed. We would drink just to get through the day. And his temper grew worse and worse and worse. He manipulated me to get me stealing with him, only I was not nearly as good. I got caught. Several times."

Her head lifted. In her eyes burned a defiant fire so hot I'm sure my skin was being singed.

"You want to know the worst thing?" Her voice hitched. "When they arrested me on my fourth straight offense and finally sentenced me, I was glad. I was glad to escape him. Since he didn't have visiting privileges, I was free of him for months. And then when I got out..." Her shoulders slumped. Her voice went flat. "He came for me. He came for me and took me...and I let him. All the while I had been in the detention center, I had sworn to myself that things would be different when I got out. That *I* would be different. And then, one look in those tender gray eyes and I crumbled."

Her hand had found mine and was gripping so tightly, as if it were the last lifeline keeping her sane.

"That night, sleep never came for me. Instead, my mind was swarming with regret—swallowed by a sudden wave of realizing that *this was it*. If I stayed here with him like this, I was not going to survive it. Even before, I had been having suicidal thoughts, but now…" She shook her head firmly. "Now, this time there would be no escaping it."

Her breathing had amped up, had taken over her whole body, all rising in heavy inhalations and exhalations. Suddenly, her head snapped to face me, and she shuddered as if the memories still terrified her.

"So, I left. I packed my bags and I walked out the door. I took the first jet I could to the US. New York City. Where I had always dreamed of going as a little girl; and my dreams finally came true. Sure, I had to go into crazy debt on my MasterCard to afford the flight, but I did it. I was gone."

Now her face had taken on a shining, luminous quality. This girl was magnificent. So young, so much heartache, yet so strong and resilient. How could I not have known I loved her?

"It must have been only a few weeks in New York, when I got word from an old friend that Henri was on his way. Most likely, he heard me wax poetic about the city enough times to correctly figure if I was going to go anywhere, it was there. So, I left again."

A grim smile.

"In the airport, the one place that sounded charming and warm and yet I'd never heard of, was

Charleston. So, I took a flight, and the rest is history."

Her body rigid, she looked as anguished as she had before she'd told her story.

I stroked a finger over her wrist tattoo and traced over the bird. And as I suspected she might, she answered my question without having to ask it.

"The sparrow is for freedom. That was what I learned from all of this. That the most important thing for me, and for my life, is freedom. Without it, there is nothing. I saw it on a poster in New York. The sparrow, the words. *N'oublie jamais*."

Her two fingers swirled in a circular motion over her tattoo as she murmured, "Never forget."

Stillness. Somewhere nearby, a bird twittered. I realized in an instant, the only thing her story had done was emphasize what I already knew. Giselle was it for me. *My girl.*

Slipping my arm around her, I eased her up. I steered us toward the balcony door I'd noticed while she was telling her story. Fitting. Like certain themes in our relationship—strawberries, public gardens—balcony talks were in there too.

Giselle snapped, "That is it? You have nothing to say?"

I squeezed her hand and drew her forward. "I have so much to say."

Once we were outside, a few breaths of fresh air

helped me focus my thoughts and the words I wanted to say. Somehow, I managed to find myself in France chasing after a girl I barely knew, yet also loved with all my heart. Had I completely lost it? *No, you haven't. You've found it.*

A blue wooden bench with chipping paint was my only option so I sat and faced her. Giselle wouldn't quite look at me, but she wasn't looking away either.

"I'm sorry about all that happened to you with losing your mom...and Henri. But if you think that changes how I feel about you, then you're out of luck."

Her eyes flickered up to fix on me.

"When I met you, Gi, you threw me so hard and so far, it was like a wave crashing over me with no warning at all. It had something to do with your easy manner...your smiles...your accent...how hours with you would flash by in a second—and it also had nothing to do with that." It was painful, getting these words out, but saying them was like finally expelling a simmering sickness that had been inside me for a long time. "All this time, I kept trying to play us down. Thinking that we were just a summer fling and nothing more. I never stopped to really think about my growing feelings for you because...I *didn't* want to acknowledge them. I was familiar with meaningless hookups. I'd just left a serious relationship that had crashed and burned. I *was* closed-off when I met you. Part of me hoped that our time together was just more of the same meaningless shit, so it'd be easier when it was over."

My hand found hers and pulled her down to my lap. I kissed her hair and inhaled again, loving that she was in my arms again. I'd never get enough of her scent—flowers and sunshine and goodness.

"And yet, part of me knew that *wasn't* the case. Things were different with you. Painfully so at times, as you pulled me out of the darkness and into the sunlight with your sincerity and laughter and joy. I never expected for this to happen to me…and yet…" I turned her face to mine as I spoke my next words. "It did. *You* happened."

I tapped her lower lip with my finger. "You caught me. Like a fish in a net. The instant you stepped out of my life it disintegrated to dust. That first night after you left…the thought of sleeping without you, or not seeing you laugh again, or never hearing you speak French to me when we made love…was too much to bear. It was *all* you. You, who made me love my life again. You, who cracked open the rigid structure I'd built around myself and showed me there were possibilities for something I'd barely dared to hope for."

Giselle's eyes were luminous, frightened almost as she asked, "What was it you barely dared to hope for?"

"Love. Finding someone to love who would also love me."

"And d-id you f-find this person?" Her eyes filled with shimmering tears reflecting the blue and white Paris sky as she waited for my answer.

I helped her off my lap and onto the bench before standing in front of her. I slipped my hand in my pocket and found the velvet box I'd brought with me. Then I went down on one knee.

"I did. I found a French beach fairy, or rather she found me." I pulled the box out of my pocket. "And I fell in love with her. She's everything I want...and need in my life. She's beautiful and sexy and funny and a wicked tease that catches me every single time. She's an incredibly talented artist, and so very generous and giving that I have to remind myself she's real sometimes. She's a gorgeous bohemian girl I barely know yet love with all my heart. She probably thinks I'm certifiably insane. But true insanity would be me not seeing the once-in-a-lifetime love in front of me right now."

I opened the box to reveal the ring I'd found in Charleston before I'd headed to the airport. An aquamarine the color of her dress set in a platinum band carved with rolling ocean waves. "So, there's only one more thing I need to know. Will you, my once-in-a-lifetime love, marry me?"

Giselle sat frozen, her hand over her mouth, her eyes wide and trailing tears. I hoped like hell they were happy ones.

She put a hand to my face and stared into my eyes. "Oui, mon beau surfeur, je vais t'épouser." *Yes, my beautiful surfing man I will*...I think.

"I'm taking that as a yes, but I think I should revisit French lessons." The smile twitching at the corner of her luscious lips was begging me for a kiss, but she still had more to say to me.

"It will be on one condition."

"Which is?"

She tugged me up from kneeling to sit beside her and looked out contentedly at the city. "Okay, okay, actually two conditions."

I gulped. If my time with Giselle had told me anything, it was that she could be stubborn about getting her way. "All right, what?"

"One thing I need to know is where will we live?"

I kissed her first, loving the taste of her lips after so many days without them, until she started making those wonderful French sounds and words I needed to hear for the rest of my life—and then I answered her.

"I will live wherever you are. We can live in Charleston at the beach house, or somewhere else altogether if you want. We can even live in Paris if that's what you need in order for us to be together. The point is, my gorgeous Gi, you are my home. Wherever you want to be is where I will live."

"I want to live in Charleston on the beach...and draw pictures of you surfing and the sea and the sky...and bring strawberries to you at work and feed them to you. I will teach you French and even pick up your dirty socks when you forget to put them in the hamper. I want to grow a patch of sunflowers for us to lie under for picnics in the garden. I want a simple life with small surprises and a great deal of peacefulness. I *need* that life to be whole again. I will come back here often to visit certainly and to see my family, but I want to *live* in Charleston with my mon beau surfeur, Gage, who I love with my whole heart."

I couldn't answer her right away. I was too busy kissing her again. And trying to keep my heart beating inside my chest.

"What's the second thing?" I asked once I could speak.

"You have to promise me that you will stay gullible to my teasing and never let on even if you know I'm doing it," she said with complete seriousness.

I swept her up in my arms and twirled her around and laughed. "I don't think you'll have a thing to worry about on that point, my lovely Gi. I'm American, so of course I'll stay gullible!"

Now Giselle was the one who was kissing me as I held her above me with the view of Paris spread out before us. "Then I have just one word for you, my love," she said.

I hope it's my favorite word.

"Oui."

CHAPTER 12

Six months later.
Folly Beach

S prawled out on the blanket in a warm bed of sand, I pulled my wife to my chest.

"So how does it feel to have a husband?" Cheesy comments had become my favorite method of teasing *her*, and the levels to which I'd go were fairly limitless.

Her chin plopped on my chest, a small smile snaking along her lips. "It feels hard and warm and rather nice actually," she said as her hand wandered over my chest and then down my abs and over my shorts to palm my cock through the material. "How does it feel to be the luckiest man in the universe?"

I laughed—something I did a lot more often now Giselle had come into my life. "Still trying to hold onto the lower leg with the teasing. I told you there was nothing to worry about me ever losing my gullibility with you. But to answer your question, it feels like I won the wife lottery. Not every guy can put a ring on a French beach fairy and keep her. It's a helluva lot harder than it looks."

Giggling cheerily, she snuggled closer, her arms draping around me. "But you did it, so good job, *husband*. It is quite fun being married to you, even if it's only been for a day. After all, think how great our wedding turned out, mostly based on my suggestions."

My hand gripped a handful of her gorgeous ass and squeezed. "Yeah, yeah, Frenchy."

Although, she was right absolutely right. Only sixty guests consisting of our families and close friends had attended the small, intimate ceremony. Reese and Gray, Reid, Reeve, Paul and Isa, who were still trying to work out where their crazy relationship was headed, Giselle's friend Brynne, who'd lived with her family in Paris as an exchange student, came out from Vegas with her husband, a handful of Giselle's local artist friends (including Nora, previously known as Old Bat Art Lady) and a few of our neighbors joined us for our ceremony on Folly Beach. Yes, we'd said our vows where we'd first met, and it was exactly how we wanted it to be. Our wedding cake was vanilla strawberry (my clever suggestion) and there was still some leftover in the freezer.

We were recovering from the party, then we'd slowly pack and get ready to leave for our honeymoon in Cannes next week. Giselle had been the one to suggest we have a break between the wedding and the honeymoon, and she was right...of course. Racing through life never gave you more time. My wife was very wise about how we lived our life. So much wiser than her years. She was an old soul in a new body.

My fingers settled on the messy knot of her hair and caressed the silkiness. "A little sparrow told me that there's something buried for you on this beach somewhere."

Giselle tossed a glare at her wrist. This was an ongoing joke between us that her sparrow tattoo liked to tell me secrets more than her. She sighed. "That ungrateful sparrow never tells me anything."

Nevertheless, she got to her feet and started walking around, peering at the sand looking for clues and digging her toes in places.

"Do I get any sort of hints?" she called over her shoulder.

"You get one stick of a hint," I called back.

Giselle stopped at the place in the sand where a long stick was jutting out and grinned over at me.

"But how am I supposed to—"

I tossed a child's plastic pink shovel her way, which she neatly caught, just as I'd known she would.

"I really have to earn this gift, no?"

Propping myself on one arm, I said nothing, just winked. I could hardly wait for the magic moment when she found it.

It only took a minute or so of gritty digging before Giselle paused. "A chest?"

Getting up, I went to sit beside her as she lifted it out. "Yeah, you like chests, don't you?"

She gave me a light elbow nudge before returning her attention to the chest. "It is beautiful."

It had taken me a few days of stealth antique hunting before I found one that fit the bill. Old looking, but not so grimy you wouldn't want to touch it. Like some impressively preserved piece you might find at the bottom of the ocean that had belonged to some old pirate captain. That was another thing I'd learned about Giselle in the past few months: one of her childhood dreams, adorably, was to own a pirate ship—but to be a *good* pirate, as she'd taken great pains to stress to me.

"Maybe it's only an old chest with nothing inside it," I teased.

"*Only* a chest. We'll see about—"

She opened the lid. "Ohhh," she breathed as

she gathered up the green fabric in her hands and pulled it to her chest lovingly. Then she stood and let it flow down as a deep sigh spilled from of her trembling lips.

"Gage, you didn't."

"I totally did." I grinned at my wife feeling quite impressed with myself.

In her hands was the insanely expensive crochet dress in a soft green we'd stumbled on in a local artisan shop downtown. The intricate twines of the crochet had been carefully handcrafted with extra-fine detailing. And though Giselle would never justify such a cost for a dress no matter how much she loved it, I had no problem whatsoever with the price. Surprising her with something perfect I'd found for her was my prerogative as her husband—as I'd told her many times.

"Don't make me wait too long," I called to her. "Let's see it on you."

Holding the dress to her body, eyes tearing up, she turned away and started to put it on over her bikini. This was another of her adorable traits. Even though we were husband and wife and I'd seen her cry at least four times now, she still hated being seen with tears in her eyes. Apparently insulting her whenever she cried had been another one of Henri's many cruel habits.

I sighed. Yes, it would take probably a lifetime for Giselle's scars regarding her ex to heal, but I was more than up to the task of helping her with that. Every time I woke up next to her, I thanked God for sending her to find me. That's what I believed, so it became my truth. She had been sent from heaven or somewhere to find me...and save me. *To be mine. Forever.*

When she returned, my jaw literally dropped. Mind. Completely. Blown.

The crochet dress looked like it had been constructed with her body in mind. The placement of every finely woven hole was perfection incarnate my fingers itched to sink into.

She cocked her hip. "What do you think?"

"Crochet is *definitely* your thing."

"You think?" she asked, all arched brow innocence.

In one swift motion, I hoisted her up, so her legs could wrap around my torso.

"I know," I said, a second before my lips crashed into hers.

The rest was preordained.

I walked us off the beach and back inside the house as fast as I could get us there.

The urge to feel and kiss every crochet-exposed hole, every delectable piece of bare skin, was my only driving need right now. My lips were drawn to the nub of her nipple spiking through her suit and the crochet, while my hands danced up and down her beautiful body, stroking to claim all the parts of it I was able.

Giselle's hands went to work on my board shorts, undoing them but not taking them off...yet.

Disengaging herself with a taunting smile, she stepped back and slowly reached down to grab hold of the hem before pulling her new dress up over her head carefully. "I don't want to snag this beautiful thing. I love it so much, but I love you more for giving it to me." I waited while she folded it and carefully placed it on the back of the chaise.

We weren't going to make it upstairs to our bedroom before we started fucking. The couch had worked for us the first time, and it had *definitely* been used plenty of times since then, so it would do perfectly now.

Adrenaline spiked in my blood as she came forward to meet me, her hands at the back of her neck pulling the tie of her bikini top. A move she had perfected to an incredible degree of sexiness by the way. As it fell to reveal the perfect tits I worshipped as often as I got the opportunity, she had managed to get the tie at her back undone so the whole top dropped with a soft swish to the floor.

Jesus.

"OH, OUT." The words spilled out of her lips as my

tongue made love to her clit.

That was when I really got to work. Feasting on my wife's pleasure, spurring her release forward, pushing her for more upon more. Every part of me hyperfocused on this one goal, this one act. To hear and feel her sweet body lose it under me.

So, I took my time, but just enough so her release would be continuous. I swirled my tongue and fingers in perfect tandem, to a subterranean beat. Our bodies grooved together. Her hips thrust against me as her head dug back into the cushions, all while moaning decadently in French.

Until the shaking of her body became sporadic. A reaction to what she couldn't hold back any longer. The piercing pleasure I was sucking and ramming into her at top, deep-stroking speed. And then she came. Her body flailed up, and then collapsed back, the shakes taking over her, becoming her, and finally, finishing with her.

Then was I settling myself over her. Our lips found each other.

Yes, *it was time*.

Our lips were the first to meet, but when my cock kissed her wet slit, that was when the real shuddering began. It was nothing short of life-giving. The first notes of the beautiful tune that you knew was your favorite.

Before I could thrust in deeper, she was already grinding against me as another shake ripped through us, both of us clutching each other. Our bodies tinged with rapid-fire shots of pleasure and this feeling—this *fucking nirvana*. Of being with the one you were meant to be with. Being *with* the only person that would ever matter.

Our bodies moving in tandem. Stroking and grasping hands. Notes of thrills and laughs and moans. All interspersed amidst that primal motion of in and out, flesh claiming flesh. That more and more. That cresting pleasure driving us forward to the end.

And so, I kept on taking her as she was giving herself to me. We swapped positions like breathing, swapped them so many times I lost track. It was all lost in the flow. *Her* legs up and around me. *Her* hands ripping through my hair and her skin bristling to the touch. *Her* softness bearing my roughness. *Her* flowery scent in my head. Her and her and *her*.

Until I was not only fused into her, I was her. We were. And like this, as us, *we came*.

The aftermath was a timeless spell of blissed-out bodies trembling with remembering. *Fucking rapture*.

She whispered the sweetest words to me. "Très cher Gage, je t'aime."

My dearest Gage, I love you.

THE END

A NOTE FROM RAINE

*H*USBAND *MATERIAL*, THIS WONDERFUL little story I absolutely loved writing, has just opened up a big new world for the direction of my creative plotting. There are good things happening down in the Carolinas for new characters you'll be meeting shortly in new books.

Readers already familiar with my work are used to the little connections I like to sprinkle in my books as Easter Eggs for them to find. For the new reader these Easter Eggs will not stand out in any remarkable way, but if you know my other books, including the historicals, then you will find those little gems placed here and there in the words and will know them when they appear.

Reid and Reeve Greymont are brothers in the gin distilling business, and boy do they have stories that need telling. The Greymont family is alive and well in the USA, as are the British Greymonts. (wink)

You might remember Grayson Lash and Reese Pinkarver from *Capitol South*, the novella I put in the

Love In Transit anthology last year—they are getting their own book called *Lovely Pink*. Reese is a cousin to Gage...who is close friends with Grayson Lash...who made a small appearance in *Husband Material*.

Even my hero, Gage, has a connection to my historical: *The Undoing of a Libertine*. How, you ask? Well, remember the boy that Jeremy hired to help him find Georgina—Danny the London street urchin who did not even know his last name? After Jeremy and Georgina brought Danny into the family, he grew up and eventually emigrated to America with Jeremy's younger brother, Revé Greymont. The two of them started the American branch of the London shipping business Jeremy owned. Since Danny didn't know his last name, he was given Danielson for a surname. Gage Danielson is his direct descendant. And just so you know...Gage has a LOT of cousins out there, so there are more connections coming in new books down the road.

Exciting times ahead.

RAINE XO

ABOUT THE AUTHOR

RAINE HAS BEEN READING ROMANCE NOVELS since she picked up that first Barbara Cartland paperback at the tender age of thirteen. She thinks it was The Flame is Love from 1975. And it's a safe bet she'll never stop reading romance novels because now she writes them too. Granted, Raine's stories are edgy enough to turn Ms. Cartland in her grave, but to her way of thinking, a tall, dark and handsome hero never goes out of fashion. Never! Writing sexy romance stories pretty much fills her days now. Raine has a prince of a husband and two brilliant sons…and two very bouncy but beloved Italian greyhounds to pull her back into the real world if the writing takes her too far away. Her sons know she likes to write stories but have never asked to read any. (Thank God.) The greyhounds are usually in her lap while she writes the stories, unfortunately both dogs at the same time. She loves to hear from readers and chat about the characters in her books. You can connect with Raine on Facebook in her **Raine Miller Romance Readers** group as she's there most every day.